"I don't want to be engaged to you, Reece!"

Reece watched her twist the ring on her finger. "I want to continue the engagement," he told her gravely. "I have to make you see how wrong you were to settle for second best, for looking for companionship instead of love."

"And I'll learn that with you, will I?" Laurel sounded skeptical.

"You're already learning it. Don't look so worried. The romantic I know is in you is going to love the romantic in me."

"Reece, I can't. . . . "

"Don't try to fight it," he warned her. "You belong to me now, Laurel. Until you accept how wrong it would have been to marry Giles. Until I say otherwise."

The arrogance of him to try to straighten out her life to his satisfaction—until he said otherwise!

CAROLE MORTIMER, one of our most popular—and prolific—English authors, began writing for the Harlequin Presents series in 1979. She now has more than forty top-selling romances to her credit and shows no signs whatsoever of running out of plot ideas. She writes strong traditional romances with a distinctly modern appeal, and her winning way with characters and romantic plot twists has earned her an enthusiastic audience worldwide.

Books by Carole Mortimer

These books may be available at your local bookseller.

Don't miss any of our special offers. Write to us at the following address for information on our newest releases.

Harlequin Reader Service
901 Fuhrmann Blvd.
P.O. Box 1325, Buffalo, NY 14269
Canadian address: P.O. Box 2800, Postal Station A,
5170 Yonge St., Willowdale, Ont. M2N 6J3

CAROLE MORTIMER

knight's possession

Harlequin Books

TORONTO • NEW YORK • LONDON
AMSTERDAM • PARIS • SYDNEY • HAMBURG
STOCKHOLM • ATHENS • TOKYO • MILAN

She turned sharply to the door at the sound of that mocking drawl, frowning at Reece as he leant against the door-frame. 'How did you get in?' she snapped.

He shrugged, strolling into the room. 'Your assistant let me in on her way out.'

Laurel bristled resentfully, as she always did around this man. 'I'm glad you approve of the decorations we have up in the shop,' she answered his opening comment.

He picked up a book on French artists from her desk and began to flick through it. 'I wasn't referring to the decorations, I was talking about the way you were smiling gleefully as you counted the money you had made today.' He paused at one of the pages in the book. 'I prefer my women a little slimmer than this, but she certainly is a sexy lady.'

Laurel snatched the book out of his hands, looking down at the page he had lingered over; the black-eyed gypsy-looking woman stood naked in front of a mirror, her well-endowed body fully upstanding. 'This has been put by for a customer,' she explained its presence on her desk, closing the book with a firm snap.

'Your Scrooge act is getting even more realistic,' Reece mocked as he sat on the side of her desk, still wearing the dark business suit of this afternoon.

'You have nothing to worry about,' Laurel scorned. 'You aren't in the least like kind, affable Bob Cratchit. And I was smiling just now because I was thinking about my party tonight, not the money I've taken today.'

CAROLE MORTIMER

knight's possession

Harlequin Books

TORONTO • NEW YORK • LONDON
AMSTERDAM • PARIS • SYDNEY • HAMBURG
STOCKHOLM • ATHENS • TOKYO • MILAN

For John, Matthew and Joshua

———————◆———◆———————

Harlequin Presents first edition April 1986
ISBN 0-373-10877-X

Original hardcover edition published in 1985
by Mills & Boon Limited

CHAPTER ONE

LAUREL placed the last paperback book on the display before ruefully draping the glittering length of silver and green tinsel so that it didn't obscure the front cover of the new blockbuster of the reigning king of adventure stories. How could you make a bookstore window look Christmassy anyway? She had tried several weeks ago to give the window some of the festive appearance of the other shops along the street, but she had to admit it hadn't been very successful, a few strategically sprayed bursts of artificial snow—that was going to be hell to get off when the time came!—a few decorations and sprigs of holly, did not make a Christmas display. Luckily books sold this time of year without that added incentive, and this delayed paperback would quickly be sold out before Christmas.

She sat back to admire the display, the person standing on the other side of the glass catching her gaze. Catching her gaze? Polly, her assistant, was leaping up and down in an effort to try and attract her attention!

Laurel frowned at her as Polly kept talking and frantically pointing, colour entering her cheeks as she saw they were attracting quite a crowd by their antics. She gave an embarrassed shrug, motioning to Polly to come inside and explain to her. She wanted people to look in the window, but not at her!

She crawled backwards on her hands and knees to the small door at the back of the window, ignoring the people who still gawked at her as she tried to manoeuvre out of the small space she had left for herself when she arranged the displays.

'Laurel, your brother is here to see you,' Polly told her breathlessly.

She narrowly avoided the display of hardbacks at the back of the window, cursing the publishing company for this late distribution of the paperback that had necessitated her disturbing the window. 'It can't be my brother,' she dismissed curtly as she felt the floor beneath her foot, easing down on to its firmness with a sense of relief, closing the door behind her, feeling hot and bothered as she straightened the black skirt she wore, brushing off the thick material the fluff from the lemon window bedding she had been kneeling on.

'Laurel, he *says* he's your brother,' her assistant insisted a little desperately.

'And I told you—Oh!' She broke off abruptly as she saw her 'brother' standing beside the flushed-faced Polly. She should have known it was *him*!

'Steady,' Reece put out strong hands to grasp her shoulders as she swayed precariously, slightly dizzy from her exertions in the window. 'Here,' he neatly plucked a piece of green tinsel from her blonde hair and held it out to her.

Laurel snatched it from his hand, at last knowing the reason for Polly's antics outside the window; obviously the young girl had been trying to tell her about the tinsel in her hair. 'Reece,' she greeted tightly, blue eyes flashing as she turned to her assistant. 'Shouldn't one of us be seeing to the customers?' she said pointedly.

Polly looked more flushed than ever, hastily making her excuses.

Laurel turned angrily back to Reece. 'Why are you here?' she demanded icily. 'As you can see, I'm very busy,' she added impatiently.

He nodded, looking around the crowded shop. 'Business looks brisk.'

'It is,' she acknowledged tersely. 'So I really don't have any time to waste . . .?'

'We can't talk here——'

Her gaze sharpened. 'Is it Amanda?'

'Would you really care?' Reece drawled derisively. 'When was the last time you saw your mother? Two months ago, wasn't it?' He arched a dark brow.

Her mouth tightened. 'I don't believe my relationship with Amanda is any of your business,' she told him coldly.

'Or lack of it,' he mocked, his firmly chiselled mouth twisting scornfully. 'But, Laurel, I am your brother.'

'You——'

'Could we get out of here?' His terse request showed he had tired of the game, scowling as a customer pushed past him on her way to the till. 'I don't want to discuss personal family business in this crowd. It's almost one-thirty, don't you have a lunch-break coming up?'

She gave him a contemptuous look. 'It's only a

week to Christmas, our busiest time of the year, *no one* in a shop takes lunch-breaks,' she derided. 'Not if they want to take the money.'

'And is that so important to you?' His golden-brown eyes narrowed.

She gave a harsh laugh. 'A *banker* asks me that? Without money *you* wouldn't be in business.'

'But the making of it isn't more important to me than my family,' he told her hardly. 'And whether you like it or not you are part of that family.'

Laurel stiffened. 'I don't have a family,' she dismissed harshly. 'Now if you'll excuse me,' she frowned worriedly as Polly began to look very harassed as she continued to take money at the till, 'I really do have to get back to work.'

Reece grasped her arm as she would have walked away from him without a second glance. 'And I *really* have to talk to you;' he bit out. 'I'll come back once you're closed this evening.'

It was a statement, not a request, and with a disinterested shrug Laurel walked away to take over from Polly. By the time she had the chance to glance up again Reece had gone.

Why had he come? She could easily have found that out if she had given him a few minutes of her time. But she hadn't felt inclined to do that. Reece was a man who told people to 'jump' and didn't even take the time to see if they did so; he knew that they would! But this was her shop, her living, and she didn't 'jump' for anyone.

'See you later tonight,' Polly came into the office to say good night once the shop had closed for the day, Laurel sitting at her desk doing the books, the other woman lingering in the doorway.

And Laurel knew why she was lingering. The younger woman had been giving her curious looks all afternoon, obviously waiting for an explanation about Reece's claim of being her brother. Laurel hadn't given her one, and she didn't give her one now either.

'Fine,' she gave a bright smile. 'About eight.'

'Yes,' Polly confirmed absently. 'Er——'

'I'd better get finished here if I want to be ready on time,' Laurel cut in firmly. 'I have to go home and take a shower before I get ready for the party.'

Polly nodded, her disappointment showing in her deep brown eyes. 'See you later, then.'

Laurel was vaguely aware of the bell on the door ringing as the other woman let herself out, a smile curving her lips as she thought of the dress she was going to wear that evening. It's royal-blue colour deepened her eyes, made her short blonde hair look like gold, the straightness of the gown's style emphasising her small uptilted breasts, narrow waist and hips. At only five feet in height she had always considered her figure too slender to be really alluring, but the silky dress showed what curves she did have to advantage. There wasn't a lot she could do to enhance her gamin features, her face dominated by big blue eyes, her nose short and slightly snub, her mouth curving, her chin small and pointed. But the dress definitely made her look sexy. Giles was going to love it!

'Very seasonal.'

She turned sharply to the door at the sound of that mocking drawl, frowning at Reece as he leant against the door-frame. 'How did you get in?' she snapped.

He shrugged, strolling into the room. 'Your assistant let me in on her way out.'

Laurel bristled resentfully, as she always did around this man. 'I'm glad you approve of the decorations we have up in the shop,' she answered his opening comment.

He picked up a book on French artists from her desk and began to flick through it. 'I wasn't referring to the decorations, I was talking about the way you were smiling gleefully as you counted the money you had made today.' He paused at one of the pages in the book. 'I prefer my women a little slimmer than this, but she certainly is a sexy lady.'

Laurel snatched the book out of his hands, looking down at the page he had lingered over; the black-eyed gypsy-looking woman stood naked in front of a mirror, her well-endowed body fully upstanding. 'This has been put by for a customer,' she explained its presence on her desk, closing the book with a firm snap.

'Your Scrooge act is getting even more realistic,' Reece mocked as he sat on the side of her desk, still wearing the dark business suit of this afternoon.

'You have nothing to worry about,' Laurel scorned. 'You aren't in the least like kind, affable Bob Cratchit. And I was smiling just now because I was thinking about my party tonight, not the money I've taken today.'

'Ah yes, the party,' Reece sobered. 'That's what I wanted to talk to you about.'

Laurel stiffened warily. 'You weren't invited.'

'No,' he acknowledged raspingly. 'But Amanda and my father were. Eventually.'

Her head went back challengingly at the rebuke she sensed in his words. 'Yes?'

'To your engagement party.' His eyes were narrowed. 'To a man they haven't even met.'

'I'm over the age of consent,' she snapped.

'Well over,' he agreed harshly. 'But all the same, I would have thought courtesy would have meant you gave your own mother a little more notice of your engagement than this morning!'

She became flushed at the condemnation, still smarting because he had implied that she was old at only twenty-six! 'I sent the invitation four days ago,' she bit out. 'I can't be held responsible for the Christmas post delaying its arrival.'

'Four days,' Reece repeated icily. 'And how long have you been planning the party?'

'A couple of months. But——'

'And when did the other invitations go out?' he persisted harshly.

'Six weeks ago. But, Reece, I don't think any of this is——'

'And when did Gilbraith's family receive their invitations?'

'They didn't,' she was able to tell him with satisfaction. 'All of Giles's family live in Scotland, and will be coming down for the wedding next summer. Which was the reason Giles and I decided to invite only friends to our engagement party. But then——'

'Then you were belatedly attacked by feelings of guilt,' Reece said with disgust. 'And at the last minute decided to invite your mother after all.'

'I didn't feel in the least guilty,' Laurel denied heatedly. 'It must be obvious by now that my mother and I lead our own, completely different, lives. Giles and I just decided it might look a little odd if my mother weren't there when everyone knows she lives in London, too.'

'God, I'm glad Amanda doesn't realise she was only invited so that you and your fiancé shouldn't be asked any embarrassing questions!' Anger made his eyes gleam more golden than brown. 'She's really excited about the invitation, thinks that the rift that has grown between the two of you is finally to be mended.'

He was even more handsome than usual when blazingly angry, his eyes like molten gold, his harsh features taking on the sharpness of a hawk; a long straight nose, high cheekbones, a firm mouth, and a square determined chin. But his anger didn't only show in his face, his six foot plus frame was tense with anger too, the muscles in his chest and arms rigid. And with his dark, almost black, short-styled hair he looked as fierce as the devil himself.

But he didn't frighten Laurel; very little did any more. 'The relationship between Amanda and me is the same as it's been for the last fifteen years; tense.'

'Since she divorced your father. Divorce is always rough on the children involved, Laurel,' he accepted gently. 'But I doubt they would be any happier holding together two people who would rather be apart.'

'And what would you know about it?' she scorned. 'Your parents were happy together, your father was devastated when your mother died.'

'Yes, he was,' he watched her with narrowed eyes. 'And now he's found happiness again with Amanda.'

'It won't last,' she scorned. 'It never does.' Since her mother's divorce from her father there had been another marriage and numerous relationships; Amanda had found happiness in none of them. There was no reason to suppose this latest marriage to Reece's father, not quite a year in duration, would be any different to them.

'It doesn't seem to have soured you to the idea of marriage,' Reece bit out.

Not marriage, perhaps, but to the idea of children, yes. She never intended to have any.

Her mother had married John Matthews twenty-seven years ago, Laurel born only a year later. And for eleven years she had been at the centre of that family, had adored her father. And then had come her parents' divorce, her mother the one to tell her that the two of them had talked and decided Laurel should be left in her mother's care. From being a happy, well-adjusted child she had suddenly been alone with Amanda, occasionally going to stay at her father's flat. But it was never the same, a strain between them now that had never been there before. Then her father had been transferred to America by his firm, and even her occasional visits to him had stopped. Laurel had hated her father as much for that as she blamed her mother for the divorce.

Maybe if Dan hadn't been taken from her, too, she may have been able to cope with the trauma, but he had gone, had become a stranger to her, no longer her adored Dan. He had visited her several years ago on his holiday from the oil rig he was working on at the time, but Laurel was sure the relief when the visit ended had been mutual. They still sent each other birthday and Christmas cards, but the spontaneous affection they had known was gone.

Giles respected her decision not to have children, didn't want any himself, the two of them agreeing they didn't need them in their marriage. She doubted she would have agreed to marry him if he hadn't felt that way.

'You know nothing of my engagement or what really happened in the past,' she told Reece coldly. 'So please don't have the arrogance to assume you know anything about me.'

'But I know quite a lot about you,' he said softly. 'Amanda is very proud of you.'

'Amanda doesn't really know me, either,' she snapped.

'She would like to.'

Laurel sighed. 'This isn't some old black-and-white film, and I'm too old for the happy ending. Amanda and I grew apart years ago, and I prefer it that way,' she added hardly.

'Scrooge is coming back,' he gently mocked. 'Don't you know that Christmas is the time for forgiving and making up?'

'Reece, what's your purpose for coming here?'

she asked wearily. 'I can't believe you just wanted to reprimand me for not sending Amanda her invitation earlier.'

'No,' he straightened. 'My father is in New York, there's no way he can get back in time for your party tonight. I've offered to accompany Amanda in his place, but I wanted to make sure you were agreeable to the idea first.' He watched her with narrowed dark eyes. Devil's eyes, one minute dark and brooding, the next shining like gold.

'I wouldn't have caused a scene, Reece, if that's what you thought.' Her mouth twisted derisively. 'When I was a child I never knew which "uncle" would be at my birthday party!'

His mouth thinned disapprovingly. 'If you're hoping to shock me, Laurel,' he rasped, 'I wouldn't even bother to try. Amanda has been perfectly frank with us about her past relationships.'

'And you and your father have forgiven her,' she scorned bitterly. 'Having lived through it all I don't feel the same generosity!'

'You're a woman yourself now, Laurel,' he spoke softly. 'Can't you see how anyone could have made the mistakes your mother did?'

'Anyone as selfish as Amanda, yes,' she acknowledged coldly. 'Anyone who didn't mind taking their happiness at the expense of innocent children!' There were two bright red spots of colour in her cheeks.

Reece looked at her silently for several minutes, and then he gave a slight shake of his head. 'Does Gilbraith know he's marrying a block of ice?' he finally asked contemptuously.

She met his gaze defiantly. 'Giles knows exactly what he's getting when he marries me!'

'Your mother said you always used to feel so passionately about things, that you were a very intense little girl.' He sounded as if he couldn't believe that description had ever fitted her.

'Everything I felt intensely about she took away from me.' Fire made her eyes glitter angrily. 'After she divorced my father we moved so many times that even my toys got left behind most of the time. Amanda said there wasn't room for them.' She remembered the hurt of often finding, after the latest move, that several more of her treasured toys had disappeared. In the end it had become so that she stopped becoming attached to anything.

'Do you have any idea how hard things were for her after the divorce from your father?' Reece asked impatiently. 'It wasn't easy for her——'

'I'm sure that whatever Amanda has told you about that time sounded convincing,' Laurel cut in dismissively. 'But I was there, and I *know* what happened.' She glanced down at the plain gold watch on her slender wrist. 'By all means bring Amanda to the party tonight,' she told him impatiently. 'She looks young enough to be your wife anyway!'

'She should, she's only twelve years older than me,' he rasped reprovingly.

'And instead of looking the forty-nine that she is she looks at least ten years younger!'

'Don't tell me you resent her because of that, too?' Reece scorned. 'Is that why you haven't introduced Gilbraith to your mother, because he might have found her the more attractive of the two of you?'

'Why, you——'

'Swine? Bastard?' Reece easily caught her arm as her hand arced up to make contact with one lean cheek, using that hold to pull her up against the rigid hardness of his body. 'You can show fire when you want to, can't you?' he grated as he looked into her furious face. 'Is that the only fire you have, I wonder?' he mused as his head lowered to hers.

Laurel was too stunned by the action to stop his mouth claiming hers. She was going to be an engaged woman in a few hours, they both knew it, and yet Reece held nothing back from the kiss, his lips moving gently over hers, temptingly, erotically, against her soft flesh, enticing her to respond as he sucked her bottom lip fully into his mouth.

She was shaking in reaction, leaning heavily into him, aware of the hard thud of his heart beneath her hand, the hardening of his thighs as he stirred in arousal. She moved up into him, her lips clinging to his now, his tongue moving gently along them but not venturing into the moist cavern beneath.

'Show me you want me, Laurel,' he urged raggedly, his lips on her throat now.

The mad trembling stopped as she looked up into Reece Harrington's face. This wasn't Giles, the man she was going to marry. 'You're wrong,' she pushed away from him. 'I don't want you.'

He released her slowly, the gold in his eyes just as slowly changing back to a dark brooding brown. 'Are you sure about that?' he asked huskily. 'Maybe you should think again before committing yourself to an engagement.'

Her mouth twisted, fully in control of her emotions now. 'I don't need to think about anything, Giles is the man I intend to marry.'

'Do you love him?'

'I don't have to——'

'How can you love him and yet still kiss another man the way you did me?' he derided hardly.

'*You* kissed *me*,' she corrected abruptly. 'And one kiss from another man, expert as it may have been, doesn't change the fact that Giles is the right man for me.' In *every* way. Giles was handsome, charming, in love with her, and best of all, not interested in becoming a father.

Reece gave a terse inclination of his head. 'I'll see you tonight at your engagement party, then. And I won't bother to tell Amanda she only got an invitation to stop there being any gossip about family rifts,' he added contemptuously.

'Tell her whatever you please,' Laurel invited dismissively. 'I've never held back from telling her the truth in the past.'

'Then I think maybe a few of those times you should have done!'

She looked at him scornfully. 'The way that you protect my mother is touching. Perhaps if you had been the first to meet her it might have been you that she married!' she added challengingly.

He gave her a quelling look of disgust before turning and leaving, the tinkle of the bell over the door preceding its slam. Laurel sat down shakily, the scene much more traumatic than she would ever have let Reece Harrington guess, not the least of it being the unexpectedness of the kiss he had given her.

It had been because of her and Reece that their parents had met at all. Driving home from a friend's one evening last winter her car had skidded on the wet road and she had smashed into the back of the car in front of her. Reece Harrington had been the driver of that car.

Reece had been uninjured but her legs and arms had been cut by the glass from the broken windscreen, and Reece had insisted on accompanying her to the hospital in the ambulance. None of her cuts were too serious, but the doctors decided to keep her in hospital for a couple of days in case of concussion or delayed shock. Reece had been marvellous, going to her flat to pick up some of her nightclothes and toiletries, telephoning her mother to let her know what had happened once he had established she was her nearest relative.

When he came to see her the next day he had missed meeting her mother by only a few minutes, and knowing Amanda as well as she did she had been glad of that. Once her mother got her claws into a man he didn't usually escape until she wanted him to.

Reece had telephoned the next morning, explaining he wouldn't be able to get in to see her that afternoon because of a business meeting, but he had asked his father to come instead and would come himself that evening. She had

protested against the need for his father to visit
her when he was probably as busy a man as Reece
himself was. But Reece had been adamant. The
gentleness and warm charm she had associated
with Reece had revealed a will of iron at that
moment.

Robert Harrington was an older, just as
charming, and just as steely, version of his son.
She had known by the expression on her
mother's face when he entered the hospital room
that his days as a single man were numbered.
They were married within the month, and Reece
Harrington had become her stepbrother. Laurel
had avoided all of them during the following year
whenever she could.

The small band played in one corner of the
room, the delicious buffet was arranged in
another; the private reception room at this
leading hotel filled with friends of Laurel and
Giles. To be truthful most of them were
Laurel's friends, the people Giles had invited
only acquaintances from the firm he worked
for. He had only been in London for about
eighteen months and so had not made a lot of
friends of his own. But he got on with most of
Laurel's friends, and had made them his own.

He was late. One of the people he worked with
had told her they thought he might still be
working, that he had been when she left. Laurel
had tried calling, but as most of the building had
already closed down for the night the switchboard
was also closed down. Still, she wasn't too
concerned just yet; the party wasn't really due to

start until eight o'clock, although almost everyone seemed to have arrived already.

The management of the hotel had made a nice job of decorating the room, and a lovely iced cake stood in the middle of the buffet table, 'Happy Engagement' written on it's top. She even had the ring in her handbag, having picked it up from the jewellers on her way to work this morning, it having needed to be made smaller. It was Giles' grandmother's ring, a ruby surrounded by large diamonds, and although Laurel found the setting a little old-fashioned she had been honoured when Giles told her it had belonged to his grandmother.

But where was he? It was getting dangerously close to eight o'clock, and he still hadn't arrived.

'You look lovely, darling.'

She turned in time to be enveloped in the heady perfume her mother wore, receiving a brief hug. If she looked lovely, then her mother looked radiantly beautiful! Amanda was as petite as she, her golden hair slightly longer and softer in style, the make-up perfect on her beautiful face, the black dress she wore clinging to her slightly fuller curves. They could have been mistaken for sisters, with Amanda only the slightly older, much more glamorously beautiful one.

'You do look lovely, Laurel.' A hint of spicy cologne pervaded her nostrils as Reece, his black evening suit tailored to him perfectly, bent to lightly brush her lips with his. 'Where is your elusive fiancé?' he drawled, brows arched.

Her mouth still tingled from the contact with his, her cheeks flushed, a feverish glitter to her eyes. 'I hope you enjoy the party,' she murmured politely. 'Please go and get yourself a drink.' She vaguely pointed in the direction of the bar behind them.

Broodingly dark eyes studied her for long timeless minutes before Reece calmly interrupted Amanda's light chatter. 'Martini?' He took her arm and led her over to the bar, both quickly swallowed up in the crowd, although Reece stood slightly taller than most of the men in the room.

Laurel was getting irritated now. Where *was* Giles? Surely he didn't have to work this late, tonight, of all nights? The announcement of their engagement was due to be made at eight-fifteen; if Giles didn't arrive soon she was going to have to delay it.

'Miss Matthews?'

She turned sharply to the waiter that hovered at her elbow. 'Yes?' she invited worriedly.

'This note has just been delivered for you.' He thrust the small envelope into her hand before hastily making his exit.

Laurel frowned as she slit open the envelope. She and Giles had received many cards of congratulations since she had told people of their forthcoming engagement; but this didn't look like one of them.

All colour drained from her cheeks as she read the short message written inside, her hands shaking so badly that she didn't have the strength to protest when the note was taken out of her hands, Reece reading it quickly.

'The bastard!' He looked up at her anxiously,

his arm going about her waist as she would have swayed.

'He gave no indication,' she mumbled into Reece's chest. 'Said nothing when I saw him two days ago. Oh God!' She looked up at him with pained eyes. 'What am I going to do with all these people? And then there's the presents and cards that will have to be returned,' she groaned. 'I——'

'Laurel, do you trust me?' he prompted intently.

She looked up into the golden-brown eyes, unable to look away. 'Yes,' she answered dazedly, knowing she *did* trust him.

'Then let me handle this,' he told her.

'But——'

'Laurel, let me,' he insisted tersely.

She searched the harshness of his face, the determination of his mouth and chin. 'Yes,' she accepted dully. 'You do what you think best.'

He squeezed her arm reassuringly before turning and making his way to the microphone, silencing the music as he stepped forward to speak. 'Ladies and gentlemen,' he greeted warmly. 'I'm glad you could all make it tonight. I hope none of you will be too disappointed when I tell you there has been one little change in the proceedings.' The silence in the room was deathly now as everyone waited expectantly.

Laurel groaned with humiliation, dropping down into a chair as her guests remained mesmerised by what Reece was saying. A 'little change', he called it; she would have described Giles defection completely differently! He had changed his mind, he had written. Couldn't go through with it, he had added. And just as an afterthought, Could he have his grandmother's ring back!

As soon as Reece had told everyone the engagement was off she was going to hide herself in her flat for the next twelve hours until necessity meant she had to come out to open the shop in the morning!

'With the fascinating enchantment of all women, Laurel has changed her mind,' Reece continued amiably.

She appreciated his help, but as she was the one at the party it was obvious *she* wasn't the one to have changed her mind!

'Much as she likes and respects Giles she has decided, for the sake of their happiness, that she can't marry him,' Reece went on.

She could sense the pitying looks directed at her even as she bent her head so that she shouldn't actually see them, knew everyone must have guessed at the truth by now.

'I hope you'll all understand when I tell you that Laurel has realised she can't marry Giles because it's *me* she loves, and that she has accepted my request that she become *my* wife,' Reece announced proudly.

Laurel's head shot back disbelievingly. He couldn't really have said *that*!

CHAPTER TWO

SHE knew he had as people surged forward to offer their congratulations.

'He's beautiful, darling.' Heather, one of her more outrageously outspoken friends, eyed Reece covetously as he left the microphone to cross the room to Laurel's side. 'I'd change my mind, too, if he asked me.' She gave the man who had accompanied her to the party a disparaging look before walking off.

'Gorgeous,' Polly agreed as she bent to kiss her cheek. 'And I fell for the "brother" routine this afternoon,' she grimaced.

'He's a lucky man.' David, Polly's husband, hugged her warmly.

'Behave yourself,' Polly glared at him. 'If I don't hit you Reece might, and he looks a powerful man to me.'

'Darling!' her mother kissed her, smiling happily. 'What a lovely surprise.'

It was a surprise, but she doubted she would ever think of it as lovely! Why on earth had Reece told these people such a lie and landed them in this mess?

He was in front of her now, his arm about her waist as he pulled her to her feet and held her at his side, the heat of his hand seeming to burn through the silky material. Laurel stood by him numbly as he charmingly accepted the congratulations still coming their way.

She felt devastated by Giles's betrayal, knew he had to realise what an embarrassing position he would put her in by not turning up at the party they had been arranging for months. She felt alternately like sitting down and crying like a hurt child or punching him in the face! If she ever saw him again. Oh yes, she would see him again; he had said he would call around tomorrow once the shop had closed to collect the ring. If he thought she was handing that over to him as well he was in for a shock!

'Darling?'

She looked up at Reece with blank eyes, too lost in thoughts of what a fool she had been to have kept up with the conversation.

He frowned as he saw the bewilderment in her eyes, his mouth firming before he bent his head to quickly claim her lips with his. Laurel gasped as she realised what he was about to do, her parted lips seeming like an invitation to the people watching them. It wasn't an exploratory kiss like the one he had given her earlier at the shop; this time he demanded, and took when she didn't freely give. His arrogant demand made her even more angry than she already was, kissing him back as roughly, her mouth swollen and bruised when he finally drew back, her eyes bright and feverish.

'When two combustible substances meet ...' David murmured admiringly.

The indulgently amused laughter of their onlookers broke the tension, Laurel turning hastily away from the humour Reece tried to share with her. 'Please, everyone, there's plenty of food and drink,' she invited. 'We're here to have a good time.'

'We'll start the dancing off.' Reece pulled her back into his arms as the band began to play a slow haunting melody, moving gracefully to the music as he moulded Laurel to him from breast to thigh. His face nuzzled in her hair as he bent down to her. 'Are you all right now?' he finally asked softly.

'You said you would handle it,' she choked.

'And you told me to do what I thought best,' he reminded huskily, giving every impression of a newly engaged man, slowly caressing her as they danced. 'If I had told them the truth you would now know the pity and embarrassment of having to return their gifts to them.'

'And instead I'm now the envy of several of my friends,' she said disgustedly, knowing that as far as Heather was concerned her boyfriend of the last few months came a very poor second to Reece.

He looked down at her with amused eyes. 'Which ones?' he teased.

Her nails dug into his neck where he had put her arms about him. 'Behave yourself!' she frowned.

'I'd rather have you fighting me than see that defeated look in your eyes when you read Gilbraith's letter,' he said seriously.

'I wasn't defeated,' she told him stiffly. 'I was angry. I still am.'

'Good,' Reece nodded admiringly.

'At you, too.' She glared at him. 'You——' Reece stopped her tirade by once again putting his mouth on hers.

'Will you stop doing that!' She wrenched away from him.

'Careful.' The warmth of his smile didn't waver for an instant. 'We have an audience,' he added pleasantly, once again holding her lightly against him.

Laurel turned sharply to look about them, feeling the colour darken her cheeks as she realised they were the only two people dancing, her friends standing around the dance floor watching them indulgently. She quickly turned back to Reece. 'Oh God,' she groaned. 'This is awful!'

'Smile when you say that.' His lips moved lightly across her cheek to the edge of her mouth.

'Reece, I feel as if I'm caught in a nightmare and can't wake up!' She trembled.

He laughed softly as he straightened. 'That's the first time any woman has described kissing me as a nightmare! I'm obviously not finding the experience of being your fiancé as unsettling as you are.'

'Why did you do it?' she groaned.

'Cheer up,' he told her lightly. 'It will only be for a few weeks.'

'A few weeks!' she repeated aghast. 'Reece, we can't possibly——'

'Of course we can,' he dismissed her objections. 'I'm quite enjoying myself, actually,' he grinned.

Anger darkened her eyes, making them look bigger than ever. 'I'm not!' she snapped.

'I can see that,' he said amiably. 'I don't have to be the consolation prize, you know.'

She frowned. 'What on earth do you mean?'

He shrugged broad shoulders. 'Well, we are engaged. It seems a pity to waste the opportunity——'

'The opportunity doesn't arise,' she told him firmly, abruptly ending the dance. 'Ask my mother to dance, Polly is getting a little frantic,' she added scornfully, several other couples dancing with them now, David and Amanda one of them, David obviously enthralled by her mother.

Reece frowned down at her. 'Amanda can't help her beauty and warmth.'

'Can't she?' Laurel said brittlely. 'Don't tell me you *are* another one, Reece?' she derided the fallibility of men falling for a beautiful face and sexy body, oblivious of the woman inside the body.

'I like your mother very much,' he told her firmly. 'In fact, sometimes I wonder how she could *be* your mother!' he reproved.

She drew in an angry breath. 'Believe me, there's no doubt about that, *I* checked it out myself years ago!'

'Laurel——'

'I have to go and powder my nose!' She walked away from him, her head held high, looking at no one, although she knew people were watching her. My God, no one believed for a minute that this engagement to Reece was a real one!

That wasn't so surprising. She had made no secret of the fact that she was marrying Giles for anything but love. She was fond of him, he was charming and pleasant to be around, made no demands on her that she wasn't prepared to give.

None of the people that really knew her would ever believe she had chosen arrogant, sensually attractive Reece Harrington in his place!

Then she would just have to make them believe it, make them think she had been so overwhelmed with love for Reece that for once she had thrown caution to the wind and given in to an impulse, that of marrying Reece. When the engagement was broken that would only reaffirm the claim she had always made that a relationship should be founded on liking and respect rather than the painful emotion of love.

But that would never be with Giles now. Even if he should get over his attack of nerves and change his mind and ask to come back she would never let him. He had forfeited any right to her affection by the humiliating blow he had dealt her tonight. If it hadn't been for Reece . . .

Reece. She had known from the moment he helped her from her wrecked car that he was a dangerous man to be around, that any woman that became involved with him would have to give her soul as well as her heart and body.

But she had no intention of becoming involved with him, merely of letting him continue to pretend to be her fiancé. And she was about to start pretending to be *his* fiancée.

He was standing near the bar talking to Amanda, Polly and David when she entered the room, setting her shoulders determinedly as she walked over to his side. 'I hope I wasn't gone too long, darling.' She stretched up to kiss him, even the high heels on her shoes meaning she still had to go a long way to reach his lips. 'I missed you,' she told him throatily.

Humour glinted in his eyes as he quickly masked his surprise at this sudden change in her. 'I missed you too, darling.' He teased her lips with his own as he curved her body up into his. 'Five minutes is too long to be apart,' he murmured mockingly.

'Wait until you've been married almost five years,' David derided. 'Then you would be glad of five *minutes* to yourself!'

'That's all the thanks I get after becoming his child-bride at only nineteen, giving him all of my youth!' Polly gave him a playful punch on the arm, the couple more in love now than they had ever been, and looking it.

'What about my youth?' he teasingly complained. 'Have you seen how many grey hairs I have on my chest now?'

'Six,' his wife taunted. 'I counted them last night. Afterwards.'

David gave Laurel and Reece an abashed smile. 'She only treats me this way because she knows I lust after her body!'

Reece laughed softly. 'I know the feeling!' He looked warmly down at Laurel.

And she had thought her acting was good! If only a 'slightly slimmer' version of the woman he had looked at in the book illustration earlier this evening was his taste for a bed-partner then she fell far short of the required inches. What she had was all in proportion, but those proportions were minimum. Nevertheless, Reece managed to look as if he really couldn't wait to get her into bed with him later this evening.

And secure in the knowledge that it wasn't
going to happen Laurel played the part of
besotted fiancée for the rest of the evening. She
was so convincing that as she and Reece
languorously danced the night away she could
feel the hard desire of his taut thighs against her
stomach!

But none of her friends looked at her curiously
any more, and even Giles's work-mates looked
convinced by her act, Laurel having assured them
they had no need to leave, most of them
convinced that Giles had been working this
evening as a way of compensation for his broken
engagement. They had assured Laurel he didn't
look too broken-hearted, and that they were sure
he would quickly recover from his disappointment. Somehow that didn't make Laurel feel
better at all!

But her friends seemed to accept that, like the
rest of them, she had fallen into the love-trap,
that all her avowals in the past that it would never
happen to her had fallen by the wayside when
confronted with Reece Harrington. She was
content to let them think that, knew it would only
make her opinion more right when her engagement to Reece floundered.

'I can't tell you how happy I am for you
both,' her mother told them warmly, Reece
insisting on driving them both home after the
party had broken up after one o'clock in the
morning, driving Amanda home first, even
though Laurel had argued that he would only
have to drive back again after taking her home.
Reece had been adamant. 'Robert is going to be

so surprised when he gets home tomorrow,' she added lightly. 'You could have let me in on the secret before the party, Reece,' she chided her stepson indulgently.

'Amanda——'

'Laurel had to talk to Giles first.' Reece's warning look in the driving mirror as Laurel sat in the back of the car effectively silenced her, her mother sitting beside Reece in the sleek silver sports model Jaguar. 'It wouldn't have been fair for us to tell anyone else until she had had a chance to explain to him.'

'No,' her mother conceded, turning to smile at Laurel. 'When is the wedding to be, darling?'

'Give us time to catch our breaths, Amanda,' Reece derided lightly. 'We only realised this evening that we're in love.'

Amanda's eyes widened in the semi-light of the streetlamped streets. 'When you went to the shop to see Laurel about my invitation?'

'Yes,' he nodded.

'Goodness, Reece, you're an even faster worker than your father,' Amanda chuckled. 'At least he waited a week after we met before proposing.'

'But I've already known Laurel for a year,' Reece reminded.

'And suddenly realised you were in love with her when you knew she was going to marry another man! That's so romantic,' Amanda sighed happily. 'Do you realise that once you and Reece are married, Laurel, that our last names will once again be the same?'

This time she ignored the warning look in the mirror, her mouth twisting derisively. 'And it's

certainly been a long time since that happened,'
she rasped.

'Has it?' Amanda frowned. 'Yes, I suppose it
has,' she nodded slowly. 'You could have taken
Frank's name——'

'I didn't want it,' she dismissed sharply, having
disliked her mother's second husband intensely.

'No,' Amanda grimaced. 'You and Frank
never did get on.'

She had never felt the need to tell her mother
the reason she disliked Frank Shepherd so much,
of the advances he always made to her whenever
she came home from the expensive boarding-
school they had sent her to after their marriage.
She had been on the edge of sixteen at the time,
just budding into womanhood, a late developer
physically, and Frank had obviously found the
way that she was developing extremely erotic.

'Frank was a——'

'We'll get straight off if you don't mind,
Amanda,' Reece cut in tightly as he stopped the
Jaguar outside the impressive Harrington home,
several lights glowing welcomingly inside the
house. 'Laurel has to open the shop in the
morning.'

'Of course, darling.' Amanda got out of the car
as Reece opened the door for her, turning to push
the seat forward so that Laurel could get out.
'I'm sure you want to sit next to Reece,' she said
knowingly.

As Laurel had been the one to insist her
mother be the one to sit next to him on the drive
here that assumption was completely erroneous.
She reluctantly climbed out of the back of the

car, receiving a hug from her mother before
getting into the front passenger seat.

'The two of you must come to dinner
tomorrow evening,' Amanda invited eagerly.
'Robert will insist,' she added firmly as Laurel
seemed about to refuse.

'And as Dad's even more arrogant than I am
we might as well give in gracefully,' Reece
accepted lightly. 'About seven-thirty, okay,
Laurel?'

'Fine,' she agreed drily, staring out the front
window as Reece walked her mother into the
house.

'What did he do to you?'

Laurel turned to give Reece a startled look, the
question coming out of the blue after they had
driven in silence for the last ten minutes. 'Giles?'
she frowned her puzzlement. 'You read the
letter——'

'Not Gilbraith,' Reece dismissed harshly.
'Frank Shepherd!'

Her breathing suddenly became ragged. 'I
rarely saw him, I was away at school a lot.'

'And when you weren't?' he persisted grimly.

She shrugged. 'I don't know——'

'Laurel, don't lie to me; I could clearly see
your face in the driving-mirror.' His hands
tightly gripped the steering-wheel, his body
rigid. 'What did the bastard do to you?' he
asked again.

She swallowed hard, moistening stiff lips.
'Amanda was only married to him for a year——'

'Laurel,' Reece cut in with controlled violence.
'I could see the disgust in your face, a

remembered fear in your eyes. Darling, tell me,' he encouraged throatily. 'It will be all right.'

She sighed. 'He didn't really do anything,' she shook her head. 'Not really.'

'Then tell me!'

'He ... it was just talk, mainly! About my body.' She looked down at her hands. 'I was just developing breasts.' She swallowed again. 'And he—he was offensive, Reece, that's all,' she dismissed impatiently.

'Did he touch you?'

She gasped at the bluntness of the query, glad of the semi-darkness to hide her flushed cheeks. 'Only once or twice,' she admitted in a pained voice. 'Look, Reece, I don't——'

'Do you know why Amanda divorced him?' Reece asked harshly.

Laurel shrugged uninterestedly. 'She told me they had realised they weren't suited to each other.'

He nodded. 'That was part of it. She stayed with him to try and give you a stable life, the education you deserved. I'm sure that if she had any idea what he was doing to you——'

'I didn't tell her then, and I don't want her to know now,' Laurel gave him a warning glare. 'I don't blame her for it, Frank was careful always to be the loving stepfather whenever my mother was around.'

'She had quite an unhappy time with him too, although it isn't up to me to discuss that with you. What a damned mess!' he ground out. 'Has—did the experience put you off making love?'

'No,' she answered abruptly. How could she be

put off something she had never been on! She had been prepared to be a wife to Giles, but he hadn't been all that interested in the physical side of their relationship either, had never tried to make love to her fully. It had been something else about him that she liked and approved of.

'Thank God,' Reece sighed his relief at her answer.

'Why didn't you let me tell Amanda the engagement wasn't a real one?' she abruptly changed the subject.

'I didn't think you would want to be the object of her pity any more than you did anyone else's,' he rasped. 'Less so than most!'

She blushed at the truth of that. 'Thank you. I—I don't think I said this earlier, but——'

'You didn't,' he mocked.

Laurel glared at him. 'You have no idea what I'm going to say!'

'I don't?' He raised innocent brows. 'I thought you were going to thank me for becoming your fiancé and so rescuing you from an awkward situation.'

'I was,' she snapped.

'Well?' he prompted as no gratitude was forthcoming.

'I said I *was*; I changed my mind!'

Reece began to laugh softly. 'Laurel, has anyone told you that you're adorable?'

No one ever had. She hadn't been a pretty child, a late developing adolescent, was now a capable lady rather than a sexy one. 'Not lately,' she drawled. 'Although I'm glad you find me so amusing,' she added with obvious sarcasm.

He sobered instantly. 'I'm not laughing at *you*, Laurel, I'm laughing at your *humour*. I like it.'

'It isn't something I'm renowned for,' she scorned drily.

'That's why it's all the more refreshing when it does surface.' He began to frown. 'What are you going to do about Giles?'

She managed to keep up with his change of thought this time, glad the subject of her unhappy experience with Frank Shepherd had been forgotten. She had never forgotten it, was surprised she had told Reece about it. But then he seemed to bring out a lot of reactions from her that weren't strictly normal for Laurel Matthews. 'I don't think I have to do anything about Giles; he seems to have already done it.'

'So it's over between the two of you, just like that?' he said disbelievingly.

'It would seem so,' she nodded abruptly, still raw from the betrayal.

'No loose ends to tie up? No broken heart to be mended?'

'My heart is my affair,' she snapped. 'And there aren't any loose ends that I can see,' she frowned.

'What about the ring he asked for?'

'If he wants it he'll have to come and get it,' she bit out tightly, thinking of the unfinished business with Giles that she didn't want to discuss with Reece.

'Tomorrow evening,' Reece nodded slowly. 'I'll make sure I'm there.'

'Why?' Her eyes widened indignantly.

'Because I don't think you should be alone with him!'

She gave a scornful laugh. 'Reece, until a few hours ago I was going to marry the man; he won't harm me,' she dismissed assuredly.

'That isn't the reason I don't want you to be alone with him.' He shook his head, his mouth firm.

'Then why——' She paled at the look in his eyes as he parked the car outside her home before turning in his seat to look at her. 'Reece, this engagement isn't real! It's just a face-saver for me until *we* can break off our engagement.'

'I know that,' he nodded. 'And so will Gilbraith if I'm not with you tomorrow.'

'He won't know we're even engaged,' she protested.

'Some of the people there tonight were *his* colleagues,' Reece reminded tautly. 'One of them is probably telephoning him right now with the news that you announced your engagement to *me*. The whole charade will have been a waste of time if he discovers it isn't real. And then we're both going to look twice as foolish.'

He was right, of course, it didn't take a genius to work it out. And why not let Giles think his defection had affected her so little she had immediately become engaged to a man who was twice the man he would ever be? If Reece were agreeable, and he obviously was, why not?

'He said he would be over once I've closed the shop for the night, that's about six-thirty,' she told Reece abruptly.

'Fine,' he nodded. 'I'll be there.'

And Laurel knew that Giles would be at the shop by six so that gave her half an hour to talk to him alone!

Reece got out of the car to open the door for her. 'I'll walk you inside.'

She didn't argue, knowing that it would have no effect if she did; Reece would do exactly what he wanted to do. He held her elbow on the way up in the lift, taking the key from her hand to unlock the door to go in and switch on the lights before she entered.

'How do you think I manage every other evening?' she mocked his protective action, throwing her bag down into a chair.

'Alone,' he bit out grimly. 'Why didn't you accept the invitation to move in with us?'

Her mouth twisted. 'Because I'm a grown woman, not a child. I run my own business and my own life. I have no intention of moving back in with my *mother*,' she derided.

'If that's a dig at me I have my own wing of the house,' he drawled.

'You still live with your father and my mother, take your meals with them,' she dismissed.

He looked at her unblinkingly. 'I'm not about to justify myself to you,' he told her coldly. 'I live there because it's my home. Now come here——'

'What . . .'

'You deliberately moved provocatively against me on the dance floor tonight.' His arms moved about her tightly as he effortlessly moulded her body to his. 'Now it's time to pay up on those promises.'

'Reece . . .'

'I've discovered the fire in you, Laurel,' he grated. 'And I intend to burn in it!'

His words made *her* feel on fire, never having been the recipient of such earthy compliments before. He had kissed her this evening several times, with varying degrees of emotion, she couldn't help but feel curious now about how it would be to be kissed by him with sensual intensity.

The kiss began as a slow exploration, but as the warmth spread through her body and she moved searchingly against him the kiss became subtly different, demanding, arousing; Laurel's hands moving restlessly over the warmth of his back beneath the evening jacket.

She had never felt in the least curious about any man's body, found Giles's light lovemaking only mildly interesting. But she was more than just curious about Reece's body, could imagine how magnificent he would look naked, her senses heightened because of her imaginings.

She gasped as the warmth of his hand closed over the material of her dress, on the mound of her breast. 'No, I——'

'Small, but perfect,' he told her huskily.

'Small is right,' she agreed bitterly, pushing his hand away.

He looked down at her with honey-warm eyes. 'But perfect,' he insisted gruffly. 'Don't you have any idea how sexy you are?'

She avoided his eyes. 'Frank said——'

'Forget that bastard!' he grated. 'What did Gilbraith say?' His eyes were narrowed.

Laurel shrugged evasively. 'He isn't—wasn't, a very sensual man,' she dismissed.

'I am,' Reece told her softly. 'Very sensual. And I've wanted you from the moment I first saw you, in every way there is and ever has been.'

'When you first saw me I was slumped over the steering-wheel of my car covered in blood,' she scorned the claim.

His steady gaze held hers. 'And I wanted you.'

'That sort of want is just a bodily function. And I'm not into the *Kama Sutra*,' she scorned.

'I said in every way there is,' he insisted intently. 'Not every position. It isn't just sex I want from you. Laurel, I——'

'Would you please go now?' She turned away, her hands clasped tightly together in front of her. 'It's been a traumatic evening; I'd like to be alone now.'

'Laurel——'

'Please go, Reece,' she sighed wearily.

'Okay,' he rasped. 'I will. It's too soon for you, I realise that, but you didn't love Gilbraith, Laurel. It's only your pride that has been injured, and once you get over that I——'

'*Our* engagement will be broken and we can get on with our respective lives,' she interrupted curtly. 'I'm grateful for your help, and a few moments ago I may even have felt a little sexual curiosity concerning you, but that's all it was.'

'Was it?' His eyes were narrowed.

'Yes, it was,' she answered calmly.

He looked at her silently for several seconds, and then he slowly nodded. 'I'll be there about six-thirty tomorrow.'

'Yes.' She accompanied him towards the door.

'I don't . . . Good God, what do you have all these locks for?' He eyed the four locks on the inside of her door disbelievingly. 'This isn't New York, you know!'

Laurel shrugged. 'There have been several burglaries in the building the last few months; these locks are just a precaution.'

Reece frowned darkly. 'Burglaries? I don't like the sound——'

'No one asked you to like or dislike it,' she snapped irritably. 'I've taken care of myself since I was sixteen years old, I certainly don't need some strong arrogant man trying to throw his undoubtable weight about in my life now!'

'I hope you weren't implying that I'm fat,' he said indignantly.

He was a big man, about two hundred pounds, possibly a little less, but he was in no way fat, just pure muscle and sinew and deep copper-tone flesh. 'Maybe a little,' she mocked. 'Maybe you don't get enough exercise.'

His eyes widened, gold flames in the dark brown depths. 'I'm hoping to improve that in the near future.'

Laurel couldn't prevent the blush coming to her cheeks at the intended innuendo. 'Reece,' she began warningly, disconcerted by the sudden grin he gave, deep grooves etched beside his mouth and eyes, an endearing dimple appearing in one cheek. 'What is it?' she demanded suspiciously.

'Am I really strong and arrogant?'

She frowned. 'It's nothing to feel proud of, arrogance isn't a virtue.'

'It is when it's combined with strength,' he said with satisfaction.

Laurel was about to argue with him, and then thought better of it; she wanted him to leave tonight, not get into an argument about his virtues—or lack of them. 'If you say so,' she conceded abruptly.

He raised dark brows, grimacing. 'You want me to leave, right?'

'That is the general idea.' She stood her ground firmly as she waited at the door.

'Don't forget to fasten the lock—all of them!— after I leave.' His hand gently cupped one side of her face. 'I don't like to think of you alone here when someone is known to be burglarising the place.'

'It's a wicked world we live in,' she taunted drily.

His mouth quirked. 'Just tell me if I'm being too over-protective,' he mocked.

She knew he was teasing, but she gave him a serious answer. 'I don't want, or need, anyone to protect me.'

'You were going to marry Gilbraith,' he pointed out reasoningly.

'It would have been a partnership, not the usual male-dominated marriage,' she dismissed.

It was to have been much more than just a marriage partnership, she and Giles had been going to be business partners, too; had already started to do so after Giles had questioned her trust in him to help her. A couple of months ago, since they had begun arranging their engagement party, she had agreed to let him handle some of the bills, had even made arrangements at the bank so that he could sign the cheques for those bills. Two days ago she had received another reminder for one of those bills. She hadn't been concerned at the time, had put the confusion down to the Christmas post. Now she wasn't so sure.

CHAPTER THREE

SHE didn't know how she could have fallen for such a trick. She had grown up around the users her mother seemed to constantly be involved with, had always been amazed when her mother didn't see through them, most of them staying around for a couple of months, taking what they could, before moving on to another lovely woman in need of friendship and a little love.

She had been in need of companionship herself if not love, but she had approached her relationship with Giles with the cool practicality she did everything else. And she had been fooled by Giles easy-going nature, his unassuming manner, she knew it now as she looked into his calculating blue eyes.

They had met six months ago when he came in to order a computer book she didn't have in stock, tentatively asking her out when he came back to collect the book. Of course, she had refused; she knew nothing about him except his name, and that he was very handsome with his blond, blue-eyed good looks.

During the summer she sat outside on a bench to eat her lunch, the square where the shop was having several placed among the bushes and flowers. Giles had begun to join her on the bench for lunch, and as she did know him as a customer it would have been churlish to ignore him when he made conversation with her. She had found that she liked talking to him, that they both had a deep interest in books. She enjoyed her lunch-breaks with him, had accepted the next time he asked her out and, over the next few months, had found him to be undemanding and comfortable to be with. Maybe undemanding and comfortable weren't qualities most women looked for in a relationship, but they had suited her. And she could see now that Giles had realised that and played his part.

He was still playing that part, but Laurel was no longer fooled by it.

'I do love you, Laurel,' he told her pleadingly. 'I just—the idea of marriage frightens me.'

'And when did you make that startling discovery?' she derided, the two of them facing each other across her office, Giles having arrived at six o'clock, as she had known he would.

'Don't be hard, Laurel,' he chided in his soft Scottish brogue. 'I don't like it when you're hard.'

'I'm so sorry,' she said with sarcasm. 'I'm usually this way when the man I intended marrying doesn't show up at our engagement party!'

'I'm trying to explain——'

'Explain!' Her eyes glowed angrily. 'You could have explained last night instead of sending me this note!' She threw it across the room at him. 'If it hadn't been for Reece——'

'You didn't tell me your stepbrother was Reece Harrington,' he accused.

'I didn't know it would interest you—then,' she added pointedly.

He flushed resentfully. 'What do you mean?

'Campbells wrote to me on Wednesday,' she bit out. 'They haven't received the cheque for next year's rent money. And yet it's been debited from the account; I checked this morning.' Her eyes narrowed on him. 'I also made sure you can't cash any more cheques from that account,' she told him hardly.

'Laurel——'

'What did you do with the money, Giles?' she asked coldly. 'I suppose it's too much to hope you haven't spent it?' she scorned her own stupidity in even asking such a question; of course he had spent it!

'If you're really Robert Harrington's step-daughter what are you doing trying to eke out a living in this dead-end shop?'

Her mouth twisted. 'Last week this dead-end shop was a "little gold-mine",' she reminded derisively, seated behind her desk as she eyed him scathingly. It had been another long day at the end of another long week; she just wanted her money back and to forget she had ever known Giles Gilbraith!

'You don't have to work at all now that your mother has married into that family!'

Laurel looked at him as if he were a stranger— as she had a feeling he was! 'I told you, my mother and I don't get on.'

He gave a scornful laugh. 'I'd get on with the devil himself for that sort of money!'

Thank God he hadn't known about the

Harringtons; he may actually have gone through with marrying her if he had known of her connection to them! 'You'll probably have to one day—get on with the devil, I mean,' she said coldly. 'Now what have you done with my money?'

'I haven't done anything——'

'Don't even try to lie any more, Giles,' she told him tiredly. 'You took the money, we both know that.'

His façade dropped completely as he confidently faced her across the room. 'I didn't take the money, *you* authorised it for me to sign that cheque. No one is going to believe you were made to do that under duress,' he sneered. 'I had bills to pay, so I paid them.'

'Thousands of pounds worth?' she scorned. '*Ten* thousand pounds?'

'Yes,' he rasped. 'After all, I have a very extravagant wife to support,' he added tauntingly.

Laurel could feel the colour drain from her cheeks. 'You—you're married?'

'Very,' he grimaced. 'Pamela needs a lot of supporting. And then there's Kevin.'

She swallowed hard. 'Your son?' she guessed raggedly.

'Yes,' Giles rasped. 'Our son.'

It had never occurred to her that Giles could already have a wife. He had always seemed to have plenty of evenings free for the two of them to meet.

'Pamela thinks I'm working,' Giles read her thoughts 'To keep her and Kevin in the manner to which they're accustomed,' he derided.

Laurel swallowed down the nausea. 'Do you love her?' It didn't sound as if he could!

'Obsessively,' he bit out grimly. 'Why else do you think I whore myself for her?'

She stiffened. 'We didn't make love!'

'Because I couldn't,' he rasped.

'I wasn't aware that I had ever given you the impression that I wanted you to!' she snapped. 'I want my money back, Giles,' she told him icily.

He shrugged. 'I told you, I don't have it any more.'

'Then you had better find it—and quickly,' she warned softly.

An unpleasant smile curved his lips. 'Or?' he challenged.

'Or find yourself charged with theft,' she bit out tightly.

"And what would the Harringtons think of that? The stepdaughter duped out of a measly few thousand pounds!'

'It wasn't measly to me,' she rasped. 'And I want it back.'

'I can't give you what I don't have.' He shrugged again, dismissively this time.

She didn't have the money to replace what she had foolishly let Giles take from her, and if she didn't pay the money due on her lease she could lose the shop. 'You can't have spent it all, Giles, you must have some of it left,' she encouraged desperately.

'I spent the last of it on a fur coat for Pamela for Christmas.' He shook his head. 'By the way, the ring is hers too, so I'd like it back.' He looked at her expectantly.

His audacity left her speechless. He had made a fool of her, stolen from her, actually given her a ring that belonged to his wife as *their* engagement ring, and now he had the nerve to ask for it back!

'Your wife's taste in jewellery seems to be as bad as her taste in men!' she bit out harshly.

Fury glittered in pale blue eyes. 'You seemed quite happy with both until today!'

'I thought you were something you weren't——'

'A pet you could order about and stroke when you felt like it!' he scoffed.

'No!' Her eyes widened angrily.

'A damned eunuch who was occasionally allowed the privilege of kissing those puritan lips.' He looked at her with dislike. 'Your engagement to Harrington is as phoney as you are!'

'I——'

'I want that ring back, Laurel.' His voice was dangerously soft. 'I would have had it yesterday if you hadn't got to the jewellers first!'

She drew in an angry breath. 'I'll return the ring when I get my money back and not before,' she announced challengingly.

'Now!' he grated.

She slowly shook her head. 'Not until I have my money. And just out of interest, where does your wife think the ring is?'

'At the jewellers being made smaller, of course,' he derided hardly.

'Of course,' she smiled humourlessly. 'Then you're going to find it a little awkward explaining it's non-appearance to her, aren't you?' she mocked.

'I want the ring, Laurel,' he ground out threateningly.

'And you can have it,' she paused. 'As soon as I get my money.'

'Why you——' He broke off, looking round as there was a loud knocking on the shop door. 'Can't he read the "Closed" sign?' Giles scowled as the knocking continued.

Laurel stood up. 'It's Reece,' she told him abruptly. 'I doubt you would want him to hear this conversation any more than I would,' she spoke softly. 'So we'll accept that we're at stalemate for the moment, agreed? I said, agreed, Giles?' she repeated hardly as he made no reply.

'I'm not giving up, Laurel,' he told her between gritted teeth.

'Don't worry,' she gave a harsh laugh. 'Neither am I!'

She moved to unlock the door, could see Reece scowling at Giles even as she opened the door to him.

'Am I late or is he early?' he demanded without preamble as Laurel relocked the door behind him.

He had brought the cold in with him, although he looked nice and warm in snug-fitting denims, a thick green sweater and black body-warmer. Laurel had rarely seen him in anything but a business or evening suit, and his informal clothing today somehow lent truth to their engagement. She hoped so, because she didn't think she could take any more humiliation today.

'He's early,' she told him softly, watching as the two men faced each other across the room, disliking each other on sight. Could Reece see what she hadn't, that Giles was weak and mercenary, that he had pretended to love her, to plan their engagement so that he could steal her money from her? Did Reece pity her even more now that he had seen the man she had contemplated marrying? If he did he gave no sign of it as he put his arm about her shoulders and held her against his side.

'No hard feelings, I hope, Gilbraith?' He watched the other man with narrowed eyes. 'I took advantage of your attack of commitment jitters and claimed Laurel for my own.'

He made it sound as if Giles were the one who had been let down, and Laurel waited to see how Giles was going to react to that. She was depending on the fact that Giles would no more want Reece to know he had tricked her out of thousands of pounds than she did, and at the moment Giles seemed to be fighting an inner battle between calling Reece a damned liar and taking the easy way out and accepting what the other man said at face value. She hoped he opted for the latter!

'As long as Laurel is happy with the decision,' he finally rasped.

'Oh, she is,' Reece nodded confidently. 'And I'll make sure she stays that way.'

Laurel wondered if she had imagined the threat behind those innocent words, but one glance at Giles's face told her she hadn't; anger was darkening his eyes.

'I'm sure I will.' She made a show of snuggling into the side of Reece's body. 'With you.'

His arms tightened about her. 'If you've got what you came for, Gilbraith?' he challenged the other man.

For a moment Laurel thought Giles was going to dispute that, and she stiffened warily.

Then he gave a barely perceptive shrug. 'For the moment,' he gave a cold smile.

'What's that supposed to mean?' Reece demanded softly. 'I think I should warn you that I won't take kindly to anyone trying to take something I consider mine.' This time there was no mistaking the threat.

'I know the feeling.' Giles widened deceptively innocent blue eyes as Laurel gasped. 'I wish you both long life and happiness,' he added lightly. 'I'll be seeing you,' he spoke directly to Laurel before letting himself out with a slam of the shop door.

A hushed silence followed his departure, and finally Laurel glanced up tentatively at Reece. He looked very dark and forbidding today—until his eyes turned to meet hers. They glowed gold with desire!

'How about cuddling up to me like that again?' he invited gruffly. 'Now that we're alone and I can do something about it.'

'Don't you ever think of anything else?' She turned and walked back into her office.

Reece followed her, as she had known he would, his strides long and relaxed. 'Around you? No,' he drawled.

Laurel sat down behind the desk once more. 'How have you managed to keep your hands off me this last year?' she derided.

'It hasn't been easy,' he answered seriously.

She looked up at him sharply. 'But somehow you managed to resist, right?' she scorned disbelievingly.

'Somehow,' he acknowledged with a soft sigh. 'It wasn't because I wanted to.'

'Then what was it?' she taunted.

'The disillusionment in deep blue eyes.' He held her gaze steadily.

The colour came and went in her already pale cheeks. 'And now I'm even more disillusioned,' she rasped. 'Broken engagements tend to do that to you.' Pride wouldn't let her admit her other foolishness concerning Giles.

'What happened between the two of you before I arrived?' Reece watched her closely.

'Not a lot,' she evaded. 'There isn't a lot left to say when one of you changes your mind about getting married.'

'Are you—friends again?' he probed softly.

'No!' she denied harshly, and then willed herself to calm down, to relax. Reece was too astute, too interested in what had taken place between her and Giles to be fooled for long if she didn't get a grip of herself. 'We never will be,' she added abruptly. 'Thank you for your offer of help, Reece, but as I told you, it was completely unnecessary,' she told him dismissively, wanting him to go.

'That wasn't the reason I wanted to be here,' he said huskily. 'I wanted to make sure he hadn't changed his mind and tried to persuade you to take him back.'

'I wouldn't do that,' she assured him stiffly.

'I wanted to be sure.'

'Reece, will you stop this!' she groaned tiredly, having had little sleep the night before, worried about her unpaid lease and the consequences of that. From Giles's attitude tonight she was going to have a lot more sleepless nights before it was settled. 'I don't need my confidence restoring—or whatever it is you're trying to do!'

'Maybe *I* do,' he said drily.

Once again she looked at him sharply. 'Reece, whatever you're doing, stop it,' she ordered coldly.

'Did Gilbraith have this much trouble?' He hunched down dejectedly in his body-warmer.

'Trouble with what?' she asked suspiciously.

'Never mind,' Reece shook his head dismissively. 'Are you about finished here?'

'I've hardly started,' she grimaced. 'I have to do the books for the end of the week yet.'

He glanced at his wrist-watch. 'It's almost seven, and we're expected for dinner at seven-thirty; how about if I help you?' he raised dark brows.

She bristled resentfully. 'I'm perfectly capable——'

'I know that,' he humoured. 'You wouldn't have stayed in business five years if you weren't.'

'How do you know how long I've had this shop?' She eyed him guardedly.

'Amanda,' he drawled. 'Is it *my* capabilities you doubt?' he quirked one brow.

She smiled openly for the first time that day. 'Hardly!'

'Private business, hmm?' he made a face.

'Yes,' she answered bluntly.

'In that case I'll go home and change, come back and take you back to your flat and then we can be off,' he organised.

'I usually walk home; it isn't far.'

'It will be quicker if I call back for you,' he insisted. 'I'll leave you to count your money now,' he teased.

She was a little surprised he had accepted her decision so easily, he didn't come over as the sort of man who readily accepted opposition to his plans. But he had agreed, and she was stunned by it. Maybe he wasn't as arrogant as she had always thought he was. Yes, he was! She was sure it had taken tremendous will-power for him not to impose his will on her. Although she ignored it for the most part she was well aware of his method of seduction this last two days, and if he thought she was going to fall into his arms like a ripe plum for the picking he was mistaken! She was grateful to him for what he had done, but not that grateful. She had heard all about the parade of women in the life of the Harrington heir, and she wasn't about to become one of their number.

'Why so pensive?'

Her head ached where she had been bent over her cashbooks the last twenty minutes, all the time, at the back of her mind, the knowledge that she had nowhere near enough money left in the bank to renew her lease for the next year. She didn't feel at all like going out to dinner, especially with her mother and Robert. The last thing she needed for the next few hours was the company of this devastatingly attractive man, she thought, as he came inside the shop out of the cold. While she closed up behind him again, she found herself wishing the chocolate-brown velvet jacket weren't quite so well tailored to the width of his shoulders, or the brown trousers to his narrow thighs and long legs. As raw as she felt emotionally she just may do something silly before the night was over! And none of her was this man's for the taking, not her body, her heart, nor her soul. And she knew he would demand all three as his by right if he chose to.

'Gilbraith didn't come back, did he?' Reece frowned at the apprehension in her eyes.

'Of course not,' she denied in a puzzled voice.

'Then are you finished here?' He rubbed his hands together to get them warm. 'It's starting to snow.'

'Really?' She moved to the door once again, opening it to let in a blast of icy cold air—and several flakes of snow. It was starting to settle on the ground, already leaving a thin layer of white over everything. 'I love the snow.' She grinned her pleasure as she briefly turned back to Reece, twisting her head back to lift her face up so that several of the fluffy flakes landed on her warm skin.

'I'll give you a snowball fight later if it settles,' Reece told her indulgently as he came to stand beside her in the doorway.

Her eyes sparkled with mischief as she looked

up at him. 'You're talking to the fifth-year snowball champion,' she warned.

'God, Laurel, you're beautiful when you let go!' he muttered before taking her into his arms to claim her mouth in a sensual caress, slowly, erotically, drawing her into him.

Reece's brand of lovemaking was an unknown quantity to her, always catching her unawares— and vulnerable. He slowly caressed her back as the kiss deepened and lengthened, her fingers fluttering nervously either side of his face as she tried to resist the urge to touch him—and failed. Her fingertips brailled the hardness of his cheek, his high bones, and that delightful dimple. It was a show of mischief in an otherwise harshly defined face, and she loved it.

'Can I have a go after you, mate?' A raucous male voice cut into the heady delight.

They broke apart abruptly, Reece light-heartedly returning the boy's banter while Laurel went hastily back inside the shop, a hand up to her temple as she realised she had once again been lost to the sensual pleasure of being in Reece Harrington's arms.

'He meant no harm, Laurel,' he spoke gruffly as he followed her through to the office, the boy having gone on his way again now.

'I know that,' she sighed. 'I . . . it just shouldn't have happened.'

'Why shouldn't it?'

'God, Reece, I was going to become engaged to another man last night!' she groaned.

'But it didn't happen.'

'It was going to,' she insisted.

'You didn't love Gilbraith, Laurel,' he told her confidently.

'I don't love you either!'

'It was only a kiss, Laurel,' he reasoned.

'There seem to have been too many of them!' She glared at him.

'I enjoy kissing you. And don't say you don't like it,' he warned abruptly. 'Or I'd have to prove you wrong,' he added with relish. 'Besides, didn't you know your nose will "grow and grow" if you tell a lie?'

The sense of the ridiculous he occasionally displayed didn't fit the image of the sober banker he was during the day, and it was all the more disconcerting because of that.

'Maybe that wouldn't be such a bad thing in my case,' she ruefully acknowledged her snub of a nose.

'I think your nose is adorable just as it is,' Reece told her as she locked up and pulled on her coat in preparation for leaving. 'It's the one thing that makes me hold out hope for you.'

She looked up at him slowly as she slid the strap of her bag over her shoulder. 'Hope for what?' she asked warily.

'The little girl inside you trying to get out from behind all that logic and practicality.' He took hold of her arm as they stepped out into the freezing cold wind, snow still lightly falling, the pavement treacherous beneath their feet. 'She pops up every now and again. She's the one that wants to play snowballs later, not the one that coldly assessed every facet of Gilbraith's nature before she decided to marry him. You slipped up badly that time, Laurel.'

She looked up at him sharply. 'What do you mean?'

He held the door open as she climbed inside the car, the wind threatening to whip it out of his hand to land against her legs if he didn't hold it tightly. 'That assessment didn't allow for the fact that *he* might decide he didn't want that sort of marriage.'

'I wouldn't even have considered marrying Giles if I hadn't—been fond of him,' she stiltedly defended as he got in the car beside her.

'You wouldn't?' he mocked.

'No!' She deeply resented the sarcasm in his voice.

'In that case you've made a miraculous recovery from his rejection,' Reece drawled.

'Like you, I am not about to justify my actions,' she bit out tautly.

Because she couldn't. After years of watching her mother's gullible heart drive her from one man to the next, one relationship to another, she had decided to marry only for reasons that didn't include love. She was twenty-six years old, had a successful business, plenty of friends, but her private life was still an empty one. A husband, a suitable husband who wouldn't make too many demands on her, emotionally or physically, had seemed like the logical step to take to erase her feelings of loneliness. She wasn't afraid of men or a physical relationship with them, she just had no intention of letting her life be ruled by passion and love for a man who could never deserve or cherish it.

But Reece was right, she had slipped up badly

where Giles was concerned, the added shock of
finding he was already married showing her just
how badly she had misjudged him, that he had
never intended going through with marrying her,
that he had only dangled the idea of marriage
between them in front of her to persuade her to
give him the opportunity to take the money that
had been his objective all the time. For all of her
practicality, she had been taken for as much of a
fool as her mother had ever been!

Reece sat in her lounge while she went through
to her bedroom to shower and change. No doubt
the restful green and cream décor she had
throughout the apartment was too practical and
ordered for him, too!

She was getting a little tired of his derision of
her orderly existence, taking out a deep purple
evening dress, its flared skirt smooth over the
gentle sway of her hips and down to the floor, the
sleeveless, strapless bodice moulded to her
curves. She had seen that setter of fashion,
Diana, Princess of Wales, in a black dress like
this that had caused furore during her engagement
to Prince Charles, and she decided she loved the
dress and had to have one as like it as possible.
Its style was ageless, could have been worn a
hundred years ago or any time in between, would
never cease to be *in* style. It left her creamy
shoulders and arms bare, the tightness of the
bodice revealing the gentle swell of her breasts
above the purple silk, She styled her hair softly
about her face, adding little make-up, knowing
her eyes had taken on the purple colour of the
dress, her mouth glistening and inviting.

'I'll call the parents and tell them we can't make it.' Reece stood up slowly as she entered the lounge, looking hypnotised by her beauty as he couldn't tear his gaze away from her. 'I'd rather stay here alone with you,' he added huskily, his hungry gaze devouring her. 'And have the pleasure of *slowly* removing that dress.'

'You don't like it?' Laurel deliberately teased him, the gown giving her a reckless feeling, as if she truly were a woman from another age and Reece were her beau.

'I love it,' he breathed raggedly.

'I had it made exactly like the original,' she said with satisfaction. 'Except for the colour. Black is a little stark on me.'

'I saw the original,' Reece told her absently. 'Diana looked no more lovely than you.'

'As she has once again been voted the most beautiful woman in the world, I thank you.' Laurel gave a graceful inclination of her head.

'There's no chance of my seeing if you look as lovely without it?' Reece prompted hopefully.

She looked at him unblinkingly. 'What do you think?'

He grimaced. 'I think we had better get back to the house before I'm in Amanda and Dad's bad books, too. Speaking of books,' he draped the velvet wrap about her shoulders, 'while you were changing—and what a change!—I took a look at yours.'

'Not a torrid romance amongst them!' she teased as they went down to his car. She knew there weren't any romance books on the bookcase in the lounge because she kept her private

collection of them in her bedroom, and no man
had ever been invited in there.

'I did find something interesting, though,' he
acknowledged the absence of the romances.

'Oh yes?' It was still quite warm in the car
from their drive here earlier, but Laurel was still
chilled, snuggling down in the white velvet wrap.

He gave her a mischievous look. 'A well-read
copy of *A Christmas Carol* by Charles Dickens.'

'It is a classic,' she pointed out without
embarrassment. 'It's also one of my favourite
stories.'

'And mine,' he admitted surprisingly.

'In that case I hope you take back what you
said about my being in the least like Scrooge,' she
said sternly.

'It's true, I've never heard you say "Bah" or
"Humbug",' he taunted.

'I'm not mean with my money either,' she
flared.

'Not with money, no,' he accepted. 'The
dinner service you bought my father and Amanda
as a wedding present was very beautiful—and
expensive.'

'But?' she prompted sharply.

'There was something else, much more important, that Scrooge was mean with,' Reece
murmured regretfully.

'His affection!' she scorned.

'Now you do sound like him,' Reece frowned.

'Reece, if this is about my relationship with
Amanda——'

'Only partly,' he sighed. 'It's about Gilbraith,
too. I could tell he was all wrong for you the

moment I met him. There was no depth to him, no——'

'I'll bear your opinion in mind,' she snapped tightly. 'But considering your own failed relationships I don't think——'

'Who says they were failed?' he frowned.

She shrugged beneath the velvet wrap. 'You aren't married either.'

'Through choice.'

'I've stayed single through choice, too.'

'A different sort of choice,' he shook his head. 'I'm looking for love, you're *avoiding* it.'

She didn't like this man's perception, or his constant comparisons between her and a man who, until visited by the three spirits who showed him the error of his ways, had been without affection or charity for anyone. She wasn't like that, she *wasn't*!

'If this dinner party is going to be in the least pleasant I think you had better stop right there,' she advised abruptly.

'Scrooge wouldn't listen either until it was almost too late,' Reece reminded softly.

She reached out and touched his arm as his hands rested lightly on the steering wheel, a derisive twist to her lips as he turned to look at her. 'Just making sure you aren't a spirit,' she mocked.

'Very funny,' he smiled without rancour. 'But I take your point; who am I to tell you how to run your life?'

Who, indeed? He was the first man to ever kiss her and succeed in blocking everything else from her mind, the past, the present, the future, seeing only Reece as he drew her into sensual oblivion. Maybe he *was* the Ghost of Christmas Present; her life hadn't been the same since he had literally taken over last night. But if he were the 'Present' he certainly wasn't the 'Yet-to-come' in her life!

Her mother looked beautiful in a simple, but elegantly styled white gown, Robert as handsome as ever as he stood at his wife's side to welcome their guests. For that was how Laurel always felt when she occasionally joined them for dinner, never feeling part of the family, although the two Harrington men always tried to make her feel so, Reece always present when she agreed to these rare intimate dinners. They had always been strictly family dinners, Reece never bringing any of his many girlfriends, Laurel feeling no inclination to bring along Giles or any of her other male acquaintances.

'Well, at last the two of you have seen some sense and got engaged,' Robert greeted them, obviously happy with the new relationship between them. 'I always thought the two of you were meant for each other. Took another man to make you realise it, though, hmm, son?' he teased Reece.

'I got her in the end.' He shook his father's hand warmly. 'And that's the important thing!'

As these family dinners had gone in the past this was a good one, all of them very relaxed, Reece a little too much so sometimes, as far as Laurel was concerned, constantly touching her and caressing her, occasionally kissing her lingeringly on the lips.

Amanda and Robert were obviously delighted with these shows of affection between their offspring, smiling at them indulgently. Laurel thought she even saw tears in her mother's eyes once, and then dismissed the idea as being ridiculous; Amanda was too self-centred to cry because she believed her daughter had found happiness.

'Is there another reason, besides her divorce from your father, and the difficult years afterwards, that you hate Amanda?' Reece probed softly on the drive back to her home.

Her face flushed fiery red. 'I don't hate——'

'Oh yes, you do,' he insisted quietly. 'I never realised just how deep it went before, but tonight—tonight, I saw it.' He looked as if it hadn't been a very pleasant sight either.

'Weren't those things enough?' She gave up denying her dislike of her own mother, faced with a man who seemed to know her almost as well as she knew herself. She had often sensed his brooding gaze on her in the past, but she hadn't realised she was so transparent to him.

He shrugged. 'Perhaps at first a little natural resentment on your part, but after that the circumstances should have brought you closer together rather than pushed you further apart. It takes two to decide to end a marriage, Laurel, but I don't hear any of this resentment directed towards your father.'

'He's dead,' she said flatly, not having seen her father again after he had gone to America, informed of his death by letter, too late even to go to his funeral.

'I know that,' Reece told her gently. 'But before that, didn't you hate him then?'

'He didn't want the marriage to end, it was Amanda's decision,' she recalled in a pained voice.

'When you no longer love someone it's usually the wisest thing to do,' Reece sympathised huskily.

'I forgave her for not loving my father any more, years ago,' Laurel assured him tautly. 'It was—I can't forgive the fact that she also separated Dan and me!' She was angry, with Reece for forcing her to relive that painful time, and with herself for the emotional way her voice broke. 'It was cruel,' she rasped, once again in control of her emotions. 'And not only that, completely selfish.'

'Dan was—your lover?' The words seemed to be forced out of him.

It came as no surprise to her to know that Amanda hadn't told Reece and his father about Dan; the whole thing showed just how selfish Amanda was! But much as she despised her mother for the way Dan had been taken from her she wasn't about to betray her cruelty to Reece, either.

'I loved him,' She avoided directly answering his question.

'You sound as if you still do?' Reece frowned as he parked the car outside her home.

'Yes,' she confirmed abruptly, knowing that no matter how badly things had gone between herself and Dan when he visited her that she would always love him; that the bond between them would never be broken.

'Is it too late, or is he married or something now?'

'No, he isn't married, but it is too late,' she spoke dully as she remembered the awkwardness there had been between Dan and herself five years ago. Yes, it was much too late for them to find that easy affection and companionship they had once known.

'Is that why you were willing to settle for that lukewarm relationship with Gilbraith?' Reece rasped.

Talking of Giles reminded her of the terrible dilemma he had put her in, and just for a few minutes she didn't want to think about it. Getting out of the car, she waited until Reece walked around it, before hurtling the powdery snow she had gathered up, straight at his head. She giggled at the comical expression on his face as the snow splattered in his hair and down over his face and jacket.

He recovered quickly from his stunned surprise, bending to pick up some snow in retaliation. 'So you want to play games.' He straightened and sent the snowball in her direction.

She was too quick for him, ducking so that the snowball landed harmlessly behind her, picking up more snow as she bent down, throwing it up at Reece from her crouching position. She hit her target a second time, getting him on the chest this time, his creamy-white shirt sticking to him wetly as the snow melted against the heat of his body.

'Why you little——'

'Champion,' she substituted smugly as she once again avoided being hit.

'We'll see about that!' He began hurtling snowballs at her fast and furiously, some of them hitting their target. They were both cold, wet— and glowing, after a few minutes. 'Uncle! Uncle!' Reece finally cried, his hair so wet he looked as if he had just stepped out from under a shower. 'You are the champion!' He grinned as they fell into each other's arms. 'But I'm the winner!' he announced as he triumphantly dropped a load of snow down her exposed cleavage.

'And I'm the victor!' Laurel told him mockingly before pushing a handful of slushy snow down the waistband of his trousers, standing back to laugh as he gave a shocked cry and began trying to get the snow out again! 'Please, darling,' she taunted as a middle-aged couple gave him a strange look on their way past. 'At least wait until we get upstairs,' she chided huskily.

He looked up in surprise, dark colour flooding his cheeks as he saw they had an audience, giving up the idea of retrieving any of the snow to grasp her arm and march her inside the building. 'You little devil!' he muttered between clenched teeth, obviously very uncomfortable as they travelled up in the lift.

She looked up at him with widely innocent eyes. 'I do have a cleavage full of wet snow,' she reminded him that he had started it.

He looked down at her, a rueful smile curving his lips as he saw the mischief in her expression. 'I'll tell you what,' he said in a conspiratorial whisper. 'I'll get your snow out for you if you get mine.'

She burst out laughing. 'I thought "frozen assets" would have dampened your desire,' she teased.

'Mine are a little more than frozen,' he grimaced. 'But a little tender loving care should take care of that!'

'Ever the optimist—or do I mean opportunist?' she drawled as she preceded him out of the lift, laughing softly as she saw the way he was having to walk so that he didn't feel too uncomfortable. 'Really, Reece, you—My God!' she came to an abrupt halt just inside her flat, hardly able to believe the sight that met her eyes.

It was no longer the soothing haven she had made it, books, furniture, clothes, all scattered about the floor, nothing in its place, no furniture left standing.

This couldn't be *her* home, she must have the wrong flat. But her key had fitted the lock, and the things strewn about the room were definitely hers!

She felt frightened, invaded, and sick, in that order. She felt as if someone had probed into her private self, exposing her, stripping her bare and leaving her naked to face the world. She didn't know if she was going to be able to keep the nausea down!

'Laurel, what is it?' Reece had finally caught up with her, stopping beside her. 'My God ...'

he groaned disbelievingly, his arm coming
instinctively about her shoulders as she began to
tremble. 'Who would do such a thing?' He shook
his head dazedly.

It was no good, she couldn't hold back the
nausea any longer. 'Excuse me,' she managed to
gasp in a strangulated voice before running into
the bathroom, tears streaming down her cheeks as
she brought up her dinner.

Strong hands held her shoulders as Reece
supported her, turning her into his arms to bury
her face against his chest, stilling her movements
as she protested.

'I'll ruin your jacket,' she groaned.

He gave her a gentle smile. 'You think a little
thing like that would put me off at last holding
you in my arms?' he attempted to tease.

She knew he was trying to make her feel
better, and he did a little, but she still had to
go out of this room and face the whole of her
world thrown on the carpet like so much
rubbish. God, even her potted plants had been emp-
tied all over the floor, the pots themselves following
behind!

She pulled out of Reece's arms, moving to the
sink to rinse her face in cold water, feeling no
better, but knowing she had to regain control of
herself. But they had had such fun downstairs, to
come up here and face this horror seemed almost
blasphemous.

'Don't touch anything,' Reece warned gently as
she would have picked up a broken figurine.

She looked up at him hesitantly, blinking
dazedly.

'We have to call the police,' he explained softly. 'There might be fingerprints.'

She didn't need fingerprints to tell her who had done this. It was obvious Reece believed it to be the burglar who had broken into the other flats in the building, but she knew better. That burglar hadn't destroyed other homes the way hers had been tonight, had carried out a cursory search, taken what he wanted, and left. The person who had been in here had been looking for something specific. Like a ring. Giles . . .

CHAPTER FOUR

SHE knew it was him as surely as if he had left a calling card. And it had all been for nothing, the ring had been in her clutch-bag at her side all evening. She had decided that as he put so much value on the ring that she had better take good care of it, and had taken it out with her. It was nestled in her purse even now. She hadn't thought Giles was desperate enough for its return to do something like this.

She sat down numbly in the window-seat as Reece called the police, letting him take charge, still sitting in the window when the police arrived a short time later, shakily answering their questions. Once they gave her permission to look round she discovered that a few pieces of inexpensive jewellery had been taken, instantly congratulating Giles on his ingenuity. If nothing had been missing the finger would have pointed firmly at him. As it was he was relying on her pride in not wanting to admit she had been duped into giving him money like some love-hungry idiot, to keep her silent. And he was right, she couldn't tell anyone of the absolute fool she had been over him.

'You're coming home with me,' Reece told her firmly once the police had gone.

She looked defeatedly at the chaos of her flat. 'What about all this?' she groaned.

'We'll come back together tomorrow and clear it up,' he promised.

She shook her head. 'I don't think I can face Amanda and Robert again tonight.'

'I said with me, Laurel.' He firmly wrapped the white velvet around her again. 'I told you, my wing of the house is completely separate from theirs.'

She knew she couldn't stay here tonight, and she didn't want to be alone either. 'Thank you,' she accepted huskily, grateful for the way he had taken control of everything, knowing she didn't have the strength right now.

'That's what fiancés are for. Hey,' he chided as she flinched, 'I'm not going to hurt you.'

He hadn't been the fiancé she had been thinking of when she couldn't hold back that involuntary shudder. She had to see Giles again, and soon, but she couldn't do it just yet, needed time to recover from—this.

'Let's go.' She stood up jerkily. 'No,' she refused sharply as he would have picked up one of her nightgowns from the floor. 'I couldn't bear to wear that now he—they, have touched it.' She quivered in revulsion at the thought that Giles may have touched her more intimate clothing. She couldn't bear them next to her skin now.

'You're right,' Reece dropped the silky article. 'Let's just get out of here. I can always go and borrow one of Amanda's for you.'

She swallowed hard. 'I'd rather you didn't. They might ask questions, and—and I couldn't talk about this tonight.'

His hand was protective at the back of her

waist. 'Don't worry, we'll sort something out later.'

She trusted him, going with him docilely, the warmth in the car not touching her. It had all taken on much more threatening overtones than just the stealing of her money, and the fact that she still had Pamela Gilbraith's gaudy ring. Maybe she should tell someone—Reece? No, she shuddered, least of all could she admit to him how utterly stupid she had been.

'It's all right, darling,' Reece misunderstood her shudder as one of reaction to the destruction of her home. 'I won't let anyone hurt you ever again.'

It was a nice thought, but she wasn't foolish enough to believe it would happen. Giles hadn't succeeded in getting what he wanted tonight and so he would be back. If the ring was so important to him maybe she should just give it back to him; she couldn't bear something like this happening again. But her money, what of her money? Without the ring she stood no chance of having that returned, and she needed it desperately.

It was almost two o'clock in the morning by the time she had showered and gone back into the adjoining bedroom, one of the guest-rooms in Reece's wing of the house. She had somehow felt as if she were tainted by Giles's touch, had felt unclean, and despite the lateness of the hour had needed to cleanse her body if not her heart and soul; she could have only black thoughts about Giles.

Reece had 'sorted her out' something to wear, and she was just fastening the last button of his

white silk shirt when a soft knock on the bedroom
door preceded his entrance. 'I don't wear pyjamas,
so I'm afraid one of my shirts was all I could
think of.' His honey gaze moved over her slowly.
'I like it,' he said huskily.

The shirt reached her knees, the shoulder
seams down to her elbows, the sleeves themselves
turned back until her hands were visible,
meaning there was hardly any sleeve left showing.
She was shapeless, looked as big as a house, and
Reece liked it!

'Thanks,' she said drily. 'I could have saved
myself the expense of the purple gown and just
worn this instead!'

'Or nothing,' he smiled. 'I'm sure that would
be even more sensational.'

'*Caused* a sensation,' she corrected.

'I know what I mean,' Reece drawled, his arms
going about her waist to draw her against him. 'I
think you have a beautiful body, Laurel——'

'Please!' she gasped, turning away. 'I—I want
to be alone now.'

'Of course.' He instantly released her, his smile
one of warm friendliness. 'I'm only just down the
hall, and if you need anything, a glass of water,
someone to talk to, anything, I—Laurel, sweet-
heart, *don't*!' he groaned as her face crumpled and
tears began to flow, her body wracked by sobs.

She offered no resistance when Reece took her
in his arms. She had tried to put such a brave
face on things, but—God, she was *frightened* by
what had happened tonight. It was a weakness,
and she despised any sign of weakness within
herself, but Reece was so strong, his arms so

reassuring, that for the first time since she was eleven years old she leant on a man for emotional support.

'I feel like it was *me* he—that was violated,' she buried her face against Reece's chest, safe in the warm darkness. 'That's how I feel, Reece,' she shuddered. 'Violated!'

'I know, Laurel.' He stroked her hair with soothing movements. 'I could see it in your face when I walked in and realised what had happened. I was only trying to divert you just now. I——'

'You don't really think my body is beautiful?' she tried to tease.

'I'm sure it is,' he spoke gently, seeming to guess how near to cracking she was. 'But I'm also sure that tonight isn't the right time for me to find out.'

She looked up at him with tear-wet eyes, even the pretence at levity gone now. 'I can't be alone tonight,' she told him bluntly. 'I need— someone.'

A nerve pulsed in the rigidity of his cheek. 'You need the reassurance of someone else's presence,' he acknowledged curtly. 'Give me a few minutes to shower and I'll be that someone.'

She swallowed hard. 'You'll use my bathroom?' Just the thought of being alone filled her with panic. She knew that tomorrow she would feel embarrassed about this dependence, but at the moment she needed him.

'I'll use your bathroom,' he nodded, smiling. 'But I have to go and get Fred first; he doesn't like to be alone at night either.'

'Fred?' she frowned at the name. 'I didn't realise you had any pets. Is he a dog or a cat?'

'A rather tattered teddy-bear,' he admitted ruefully.

Her eyes widened at the thought of this man possibly still taking a teddy-bear to bed with him, the idea so novel she almost forgot about the break-in at her flat tonight. Then she realised that was exactly what she was supposed to do. 'You're teasing me,' she chided.

'Scouts honour,' he denied indignantly, making the appropriate salute.

Her mouth twisted. 'They didn't allow rogues like you in the Boy Scouts.'

'I bribed my way in with a gift of a tent for the field-trips.'

'Somehow I *do* believe that,' she nodded slowly. 'There really is a teddy-bear called Fred?' she grimaced.

'Yes,' Reece grinned, looking very rakish. 'But he's been stuck in a storage box at the bottom of my bed for the last twenty-five years, since I discovered girls are much more interesting to cuddle. My mother insisted I keep him, said I might like to give him to my own son one day. I thought I might need him tonight for protection. After all, you might have designs on my body while I'm sleeping.' He looked at her with widely innocent eyes. 'Fred will make sure you stay over your own side of the bed.'

She knew he was telling her that she could sleep untouched on her side of the bed if she wanted to, and she was grateful for his consideration. 'Your honour will be perfectly safe

with me,' she assured him drily. 'But you can get
Fred anyway.'

She got into bed once he had gone to his own
room, in control again now, although her skin
still crawled when she thought of the destruction
of her flat. What would Giles's next move be now
that he hadn't managed to find the ring? He
could only keep stalling his wife for so long.

Wife. All the months she had known him she
hadn't even guessed. And a child, too. What sort
of a father was he? He had claimed he didn't like
children, had sounded convincing in that dislike,
too. But everything he had told her during their
relationship had sounded convincing!

'Cuddle Fred until I get back,' Reece thrust the
teddy bear in front of her face where she sat up
in bed, her arms about her legs over the covers,
her chin resting on her knees.

He hadn't been joking when he described the
bear as 'tattered'; one ear looked as if it had been
sewn on several times, his mouth was slightly
lop-sided where the stitching had come out, the
button nose hanging on by a few threads, what
had once been smooth glossy golden fur now
matted and slightly the worse for wear.

Laurel gently took the bear in her hands. 'You
must have loved him very much,' she said
huskily.

He nodded. 'Thinking about it now I feel a
little guilty about the speed with which he was
dispatched to the storage box,' he grimaced.
'After years of loving me faithfully, too.'

Laurel couldn't help smiling at the almost
boyish look to his regretful expression. He was a

man of contradictions, had been disapproving
and reproving at the shop yesterday evening, had
leapt to her defence with this bogus engagement
when Giles let her down, teased her unmercifully
during this evening while still managing to
convey desire, had taken control of the situation
when they got to her flat, had been gently
supportive since that time, hadn't been suggestive
or asked a lot of stupid questions when she asked
him to spend the night with her as a lot of other
men would have done in the circumstances. He
was many men rolled into one, the friend, the
brother, the lover—*no*, not the lover!

'Maybe Fred will be enough company for me
after all,' she avoided looking directly at Reece.
'He looks the sort of bear that would fight my
dragons for me,' she murmured softly, gently
holding the ragged bear.

'He is,' Reece agreed softly. 'But he isn't too
good at cuddling.'

She laughed brittlely. 'That's okay, neither am
I.' Her lids flew back as her confused gaze
clashed with him. 'I meant——'

'That's okay, Laurel,' Reece smiled gently.
'But if I stay I'm not going to force myself on
you,' he promised huskily. 'In any way.'

It wasn't him she was worried about, and they
both knew it. *She* was the vulnerable one
tonight, daren't take the risk of those feelings
leading her into a relationship that she wouldn't
want in the sane light of day.

'Fred will be fine with me,' she deliberately
avoided the question in his eyes. 'I promise not to
try and play on his loyalty to you,' she teased.

Reece nodded abruptly. 'If you need me you know where I am.'

Laurel stared at the closed door once he had left. My God, she had actually hurt him by refusing his offer of comfort, had seen the pain in his eyes. He gave the impression of being impregnable, as a banker had power over a lot of other people's lives, and yet she had hurt him by refusing his offer of help. He was more than a man of contradictions, he was complex!

Regret for having wounded him after his kindness to her made her want to run after him and tell him how much she needed him. But the last time she had told someone she needed him and begged him to stay, he had gone anyway. Dan. And her father before him. She could manage without anyone's help, least of all Reece Harrington's!

But she didn't sleep ... couldn't ... still felt threatened. She got up to wander about the bedroom, tried to interest herself in a book from the bookcase and failed, finally taking the ring out of her purse that seemed to be the cause of this recent shock. It wasn't even a pretty ring by today's fashions, the ruby and surrounding diamonds heavy for the thin gold band.

'I thought I told you to call me if you needed me,' Reece stood in the doorway, his hair slightly tousled where he had obviously been lying in bed, the dark brown robe he wore belted at his waist, his legs strong and tanned, covered in a fine dark hair.

Laurel gave a guilty start, her fingers closing

about the ring she still held. 'I don't need you,' she dismissed lightly. 'I can't sleep, that's all.'

His eyes narrowed. 'What were you doing when I came into the room?'

'Doing?' she delayed, brows arched enquiringly.

'Yes.' He walked across the room, his hands coming out of the pockets of his robe to clasp hers, gently opening her fingers to reveal the ring. 'Gilbraith's,' he rasped.

She watched as he picked the ring up to examine it. 'Yes,' she confirmed huskily.

'I thought you gave it back to him?' He looked at her with narrowed eyes.

'I—he forgot all about it when you arrived,' her voice quivered at the lie.

His eyes gleamed golden as he looked at her fiercely. 'He isn't worth it, Laurel,' he snapped.

Her eyes widened. 'I don't——'

'I know you don't think it's any of my business,' he dropped the ring in his pocket, his arms going about her. 'But I don't want you breaking your heart over him when you think no one is around to see it. He wasn't half good enough for you.'

She bristled angrily. 'What do you——'

'Know about it?' Reece finished tautly. 'I know a lot more than you think. For instance, I know you never slept with Gilbraith——'

She gave an angry gasp. 'Whether I did or not has nothing to do with you!'

'Of course it does,' he reasoned calmly. 'If you haven't slept with Gilbraith, and you've been seeing him for six months, then it tells me I have to be very gentle with you when we make love or I might rush you when you need a long, slow loving.'

'As we aren't *going* to make love . . .' she began coldly.

'Oh but we are, Laurel,' he told her confidently. 'We most certainly are,' he murmured.

'No!'

'You can't sleep and neither can I——'

'That's no reason to casually jump into bed together!' she flared.

Reece smiled. 'We wouldn't be "jumping".' Just to demonstrate his point he swung her up in his arms and laid her down gently on the bed before coming down next to her. 'And there won't be anything "casual" about it either.' He began to undo the buttons on the shirt she wore. 'I intend to make love to you regularly from now on, at least once or twice a night, and again in the mornings.'

'Reece!' she gasped as the warmth of his hand moved aside the partly unbuttoned shirt to cup the rise of her exposed breast. 'Reece, you can't——'

'Of course I can,' he soothed. 'Of course, *you* might need to rest every now and again, being out of condition, but I can assure you I have enough desire in me for you to last a lifetime.'

'That wasn't what I meant.' She frantically shook her head. '*We* can't.'

'Of course we can,' he soothed again, pushing the shirt down off one shoulder as his mouth made a slow determined path to her breast.

'Re—*eece*!' she gasped as the hot moistness of

his mouth claimed her nipple, his tongue moving rhythmically against the rapidly hardening nub. 'You said you wouldn't force yourself on me,' she reminded heatedly.

He looked down at her with brooding eyes. 'I'm not. I'd never force myself on any woman just because I'm stronger than she is.'

'Then . . .'

'You're ready for this, darling,' he insisted firmly, unbuttoning the shirt all the way down now, his eyes deeply gold as he looked his fill of her. 'You *are* beautiful, Laurel,' he told her almost reverently.

As she looked into his eyes she *felt* beautiful, every nerve, every inch of her body, coming alive at the touch of his gaze. She knew what he would see when he looked at her: small pert breasts, a slender waist, narrow hips, legs tapered and long. Her breasts ached and the female core of her instantly became moist and heated.

'Reece!' she cried her confusion with the new emotions sweeping through her.

'I won't hurt you, Laurel,' he urged gruffly. 'I'd never hurt you. I just want to love you; you can stop me if I do anything you don't like.'

She knew he was thinking of what she had gone through with Frank Shepherd, and she told herself she would stop him after a few minutes, that she just wanted to lose herself in his warmth for a while, to feel his desire. But as his mouth once again claimed her breast, her thighs arching up invitingly, the 'few minutes' faded away and became unimportant.

Her shirt was gone now. Sitting up she helped

him off with his robe, the tug of his mouth on her breasts making the task take twice as long as it should have done, falling weakly down on to his chest once he was as naked as she, their mouths fusing moistly.

His nipples reacted as strongly as hers as she caressed the hard brown nubs with her lips and tongue, kissing her way down his chest to his waist, lingering there to delve the warm cavern of his navel with her tongue, loving the way his body jerked in reaction to the caress. She could feel the hardness of his desire against her breasts, feel him pulsating, ached to capture him into her throbbing warmth, aching for *him*.

'Reece, I need——'

'I know.' He smoothed her hair back from her face to look deeply into her eyes. 'I wanted to take this nice and slow, Laurel, want to make it so good for you that next time you want it as much as I do, but you need this now.' He pulled her above him, probing her moistly. 'And God knows I've needed you long enough!'

'Reece?' She barely had time to question before he positioned her astride him, surging into her completely, tearing through the thin barrier on his way. She couldn't bear the pained look in his eyes as he realised what had happened. 'It feels good, Reece.' She covered his face with kisses. 'Make it feel even better,' she invited huskily, knowing he could, knowing at this moment that he could do anything he wanted to do.

He didn't question or probe why she had still been a virgin at twenty-six, he just gently pulled her down to him, his kiss filled with such sweet intensity that it made her feel like crying. Then he began to move inside her, gently at first so as not to give her any more pain, and then stronger and harder as she encouraged him to do so, holding the softness of her bottom to help her maintain the rhythm they had set, looking directly into her eyes as she felt something warm and exciting about to burst from within her, her head thrown back now as the force of the explosion, within and around her, made her back and neck arch out of control. At the same time she heard Reece's groan as he gave himself up inside her, his body shuddering again and again as the pleasure seemed never-ending.

Laurel fell weakly against his shoulder, her body aching in a strange and wonderful way, the lethargy that came over her one of exhaustion rather than just tiredness. She fell asleep still lying on top of him.

Fred was tucked next to her cheek when she woke up, and for several minutes she forgot where she was, smiling at how relaxed her body felt. Then she remembered what had taken place last night.

She sat up with a jerk, Fred tumbling to the floor. There was no sign of Reece in the room, not even the robe that she had thrown to the floor so heatedly the night before, no sound coming from the adjoining bathroom either.

But she knew she hadn't imagined or dreamt— no *dream* could be that vivid!—his presence with her last night. And she had fallen asleep in his arms.

God, she remembered it all now, remembered being woken by him again just as dawn was breaking, their lovemaking slow and languid, arousing her to heights she hadn't thought existed. She had reached that peak of sensual pleasure twice more, once at the touch of his mouth and the next with the powerful thrusts of his body. And now she wanted him again.

It was beyond her comprehension that she should react so volatilely to such a man. No doubt he found her inexperienced lack of control heightened his own pleasure; she had heard men found it very exciting to be a woman's first lover, and consequently her teacher in the art of sensual delight.

Then why had he left her like this? If he had found her that exciting surely he would have still been at her side this morning?

Uncertainty marred her brow. Perhaps he had found her *so* inexperienced he had wanted to be gone before she woke up? The thought that that might be the reason irritated her into anger. It was one thing for her to know it had been a mistake for them to make love, quite something else for Reece to come to the same conclusion. He had a damned nerve seducing her and then leaving before he had to tell her what a disappointment she had been to him. This only enhanced her view that sex was a very minor part of a relationship, that once sexual curiosity had been satisfied there was nothing else left. She could at least thank Reece for showing her that, even if she deplored his way of showing her.

She turned to the door as it was quietly

opened, the curious face of one of the maids looking in at her.

'I hope I didn't wake you?' The young girl looked worried that she might have done so.

A blush darkened her cheeks; she felt like a woman Reece had casually brought home for the night! 'No, I was already awake,' she answered sharply, wishing she could get out of bed, but too aware of her nakedness to do so.

The maid smiled her relief. 'Mr Reece told me to keep checking up on you so that I could bring your breakfast as soon as you woke up, but he said I wasn't to disturb you.'

'And you didn't,' Laurel assured her briskly. 'Er—Where is Reece?' She deliberately kept her gaze steady.

'He had to go out,' the young girl told her lightly. 'Now what can I get you for breakfast? Eggs and bacon? Mushrooms? Sausages?' She looked at Laurel enquiringly.

It was all she could do not to shudder at the thought of a cooked breakfast! 'Toast and coffee will be fine,' she accepted faintly.

'Are you sure?' The maid looked worried again.

No doubt Reece had eaten a hearty breakfast before going out, and had instructed this young girl to make sure she did likewise! Feed her before he got rid of her! 'Very sure,' she nodded. 'Did Reece say when he would be back?' she asked lightly.

'No. But he did say you were to wait for him. I'll be back shortly with your breakfast,' she smiled.

'Thank you.' Laurel dropped back down on to the pillows as the door closed softly. Reece was coming back then. Maybe she hadn't been such a disappointment to him after all!

She hadn't been disappointed, she would be lying if she said she had. After Frank's perversion she had avoided all physical involvement with men, had found no difficulty in doing so, until last night. Reece didn't evoke the same coldness within her that she felt with other men at the thought of a physical relationship. Other men had tried to fight that uninterest, and they had all failed, her responses to Giles made mechanically, not even touching her. Then why should Reece be so different? Maybe it was because he had refused to take no for an answer. But that greedy sort of approach had always left her cold in the past, so that couldn't be it. So what was different about Reece Harrington? She had no doubt what a psychiatrist's answer would be, but she denied that with everything in her. She was *not* in love with Reece Harrington.

It wasn't until she stood under the shower's spray, the water cascading like diamonds, that she remembered Reece had pocketed Giles's ring last night. Wrapping a towel about her wet hair, buttoning on the shirt Reece had lent her, she made a hurried search of her bedroom. The ring wasn't there. Just down the hall, Reece had said his bedroom was. She found it on opening the second door.

It was a warm attractive room, browns, oranges, and pale cream in décor, the furniture not too austere and masculine, and the wide double bed looked more than capable of taking Reece's size and height; they had been a little cramped last night in the normal-size double bed in her bedroom.

The room was spotlessly clean but not tidy, several articles of clothing dropped over a chair, an open book on the bedside table, several pairs of shoes kicked under the dressing table. Obviously the staff had been told to clean the room but not to tidy it, the bed already made after Reece's brief rest in it the night before. Laurel's fingers itched to tidy the place up, meticulously tidy herself.

But she hadn't come here to take care of Reece's untidiness. The robe he had worn the night before was one of the articles of clothing thrown across the chair. Searching through someone else's pockets wasn't something she would normally have done, but she needed that ring if she were to have any sort of leverage with Giles at all. The pockets in the robe were empty.

Maybe Reece had forgotten the ring this morning too and it had fallen out when he took off the robe? She threw the robe back down on the chair, falling to her knees to begin searching the peach-carpeted floor. The maid had obviously already cleaned in here but there was always the chance it had fallen under the bed. It had to be *somewhere*!

'I know I asked you to wait for me,' an amused voice murmured from somewhere behind her, 'but I didn't, even in my wildest fantasy, think you would be waiting in my bedroom for me.'

Laurel straightened guiltily, still on her knees,

the towel removed from her hair a long time ago as it kept falling down over her eyes, her short blonde hair drying in the deep waves she meticulously straightened each time she styled it. She looked very young, almost childish, and her voice was all the sharper because she knew exactly how she looked. 'Where have you been?' she snapped, standing up to face him.

Reece shrugged, coming fully into the room to close the door behind him. 'To buy a copy of the *Kama Sutra*,' he teased. 'After last night I think you're ready for it!'

She blushed as she too recalled her enthusiasm for each new pleasurable act Reece had introduced her to. 'Run out of ideas already?' she challenged harshly.

He smiled, his eyes tender with emotion. 'The way I feel when I look at you I could invent a few the *Kama Sutra* never heard of!'

She avoided his heated gaze. 'Where have you been, Reece?' The huskiness of her voice gave lie to her outward calm.

'To your flat,' he revealed softly.

Her panicked gaze flew to his face. 'Whatever for?' she demanded sharply.

'Laurel——'

'Did you go into my bag to get the key?' she realised indignantly. 'How dare you go through my personal things?'

He raised mocking brows, looking at their surroundings pointedly, reminding her that *she* had been the one caught snooping about his bedroom. 'Don't worry,' he drawled at the blush to her cheeks. 'I don't have anything to hide.'

'Neither do I!' she claimed indignantly.

'No?' he queried softly.

Laurel looked at him searchingly, knowing that *he* had found something. But what? She hadn't left any incriminating records lying about, and the letter from Campbells was in her handbag, so——

'I found the books, Laurel,' Reece told her huskily.

She shook her head. 'I don't keep my cash books at the flat,' she denied confidently.

'Not cash books,' he laughed dismissively. 'Don't you ever think of anything else but work?'

As she had spent the majority of the morning thinking about him she ignored that question! 'Why have you been snooping about my home?' she demanded harshly.

Reece shook his head. 'I wasn't "snooping", I was cleaning the place up——'

'Cleaning it up?' she frowned.

'As in putting things back in their proper place,' he explained more fully. 'As you seem to be a person that likes to lie in bed in the morning and I like to get up I decided that one of us might as well be putting your flat back to some normality.'

'You,' she acknowledged slowly.

'Mm,' he nodded. 'Of course I haven't put *everything* back where it was, mainly because I don't know where they all go. But even if I say so myself I've done quite a good job of clearing up.'

'*You* have been tidying my flat?' She looked about the chaos of his own bedroom pointedly.

Reece gave a rueful grimace. 'Just because I'm not Mr Neat——'

'You certainly aren't,' she scorned.

'Don't try and change the subject with my liking of ordered untidyness.' He looked at her challengingly as he made the claim. 'It won't make me forget the books,' he added enticingly.

'What books?' she demanded impatiently.

'Big, romantic, *lusty*, bestsellers,' he revealed with satisfaction. 'They appeared to have come out of a cupboard in your bedroom.'

'You had no right,' Laurel accused heatedly. 'Poking and prying——'

'Laurel, I only put the books back in the cupboard,' he reasoned. 'I could tell by the covers what sort of books they were.'

Her mouth tightened as she thought of Giles also seeing those romantic tales of pirates and rogues who always managed to tame the fiesty heroine enough by the last page to marry her. She had learnt over the years that looking at a person's preferences in books was like looking at the person themself. Reece obviously thought so, too!

'Darling, don't look so stricken,' he encouraged indulgently. 'It's nice to know you're a romantic, because I am, too.'

'You?' she scorned.

'I'll forgive you your scepticism because you really don't know me very well yet,' he said in a hurt voice. 'But I am a romantic. I knew I wanted you——'

'From the moment we met,' she finished with weary cynicism. 'Please, Reece, spare me that. Just give me the ring and I'll leave.'

'Gilbraith's ring?' he frowned darkly.

'Well, of course, Giles's ring,' she dismissed impatiently. 'You have got it, haven't you?' she frowned.

'Yes. But——'

'Then I'll take it and be on my way.' She looked at him expectantly.

'The ring will be quite safe with me until you've arranged another time for Gilbraith to come and collect it,' Reece told her arrogantly.

'I want it back, Reece. Now,' Laurel snapped harshly.

'You can't have it,' he shrugged. 'I've locked it away in the safe. You won't need to keep worrying about the damned thing if it's safely locked away.'

'It's my ring, and——'

'Correction, it's Gilbraith's ring,' Reece cut in gently. 'Calm down, Laurel,' he advised softly as she seemed about to explode. 'I bought you a replacement.'

'A *what*?' she demanded with controlled violence.

He grinned, reaching into the pocket of his tailored jacket to take out a ring box and flick open the lid. 'I think it's an improvement on Gilbraith's ring,' he said smugly.

Any woman who didn't think so had to be insane! A simple gold band supported the most perfect diamond Laurel had ever seen, its many facets winking and glinting in the winter morning sunlight. She looked up at Reece's expectant face. 'You aren't expecting me to wear that, are you?' she dismissed.

He shrugged, looking down at the ring with regret. 'I thought it was rather magnificent myself, but if you don't like it——'

'Of course I like it. But I am not wearing it just so that people will be convinced of our engagement,' she said disgustedly. 'Put it back in the safe with the other family heirlooms.'

'It isn't a family heirloom,' he frowned. 'I went out yesterday and bought this just for you.'

'I'm sure the jeweller will be only too glad to take it back,' she bit out.

'At least try it on,' he encouraged. 'Just to see if I had the right size.'

'Reece——'

'Please.'

He had used exactly that pleading tone at the height of their lovemaking the night before, and she wordlessly put out her hand for him to slide the ring on to her finger.

'Perfect,' he smiled as she twisted the ring around on her finger. 'No, don't take it off,' he said sharply as she would have returned it to him.

Laurel looked puzzled by his vehemence, but she froze in the action anyway. 'Why not?' she frowned.

'It's a superstition I have,' he shrugged. 'I don't want you to take it off now that I've put it on your finger.'

'You said I only had to try it on——'

'Stop being so argumentative, Laurel,' he chided. 'We're engaged—and staying that way,' he announced determinedly.

'Reece——'

'I have my reasons for wanting this engagement to be a real one,' he told her challengingly. 'So it will be.'

Laurel glared at him. 'I'd be interested to hear what they are!'

He smiled. 'I felt sure that you would be,' he drawled. 'And my first reason is very simple, someone broke into your flat last night——'

'And as a result we spent the night together,' she exasperatedly guessed the reason he had mentioned the burglary. 'I'm not about to pretend that last night didn't happen . . .'

'I think I know you a little better than to think that you would,' Reece said gently.

She gave him a scornful look. 'I was about to add,' she continued pointedly, 'that while neither of us can just forget last night happened it in no way places any feelings of responsibility towards me on your part. It happened,' she stated firmly. 'And that's the end of it.'

'No, it isn't,' he told her confidently.

She looked at him with narrowed eyes. 'The chances of my being pregnant——'

'Are not enough for me to insist the engagement become a real one,' he finished patiently.

'Then why——'

'You haven't heard my second reason for continuing the engagement yet,' he pointed out mildly.

Laurel eyed him warily. 'What is it?'

'I like being engaged to you.'

'*What?*' She stared at him disbelievingly.

'I like being engaged to you,' he repeated firmly. 'I like being with you, talking to you, I like the two of us belonging to each other.'

'Reece, I don't want to be engaged to you!'

'There's another reason I want us to continue the engagement,' he told her gravely. 'I have to make you see how wrong you were to settle for Gilbraith, for second best, for looking for companionship instead of love.'

'And I'll learn that with you, will I?' she derided.

'You're already learning it . . . you were a warm and vibrant woman in my bed last night.'

Colour warmed her cheeks. 'That was——'

'Laurel, I desire you, very much. And I'm going to show you just how much you would have been missing by marrying Gilbraith or any man like him. Don't look so worried,' he chided. 'The romantic I know is in you is going to love the romantic in me.'

'Reece, I can't——'

'Don't even try to fight it, Laurel,' he advised gently. 'Last night you gave yourself to me, and if nothing else it gives me the right to continue this engagement until you can accept how wrong it would have been to marry Gilbraith.'

'I was upset last night——'

Reece shook his head. 'You've been upset before, it hasn't made you go to bed with another man, to give yourself the way you did. You belong to me now, Laurel. Until I say otherwise.'

CHAPTER FIVE

HE was insane. A few screws had come loose, probably when she pelted him with snowballs!

Then why, two hours later, was she still wearing this great rock on her finger?

She had refused Reece's invitation to spend the day with him, insisting he take her home and leave her there. Miraculously he had done so without argument.

Why was this diamond ring still on her finger? What was his damned superstition anyway, would they both drop down dead if she took the ring off? The truth of it was she was afraid to find out!

Since arriving back at her apartment it was this diversion that had kept her calm. Reece had been very good at putting things back where they belonged, almost everything back in it's proper place. And yet she could *feel* Giles's touch on everything, felt as if all her things, everything, had an unseen dirt on them, and that if she touched them she would feel dirty, too. It was as if a ravaging of her inner self had taken place.

But the puzzle Reece was turning out to be continued to occupy her thoughts. A romantic, he called himself, and yet he sat behind a desk all day in the family-run bank, being anything but that! But a staid banker couldn't have had the fun they had throwing snowballs at each other.

Although she was aware that he often hid his arrogance behind teasing, and yet no matter how he did things they always came out the way he wanted them to. He would protect what he believed to be his, and at the moment he considered her part of that, *insisted* she be part of it. And if she were to stand any chance of getting her money back from Giles she had to stop things between herself and Reece right now, needed to be completely accessible if Giles came to see her again. If only Reece weren't as insensitive as a rhino—with a skin as thick!

No matter how many times she had told him on the drive back to her flat that she wouldn't allow him to treat this engagement as a real one he had still told her just before he drove away that he would pick her up at seven-thirty the following night for dinner. He was worse than insensitive, he was bloody-minded! She was an independent woman, it seemed she had always been that way, she didn't need some know-it-all male messing up her life! The damned arrogance of him to *tell* her he intended treating their engagement as a real one until he decided otherwise. One night together and he thought he had the right to try and straighten out her life to his satisfaction, to be the white knight of every woman's dreams. He should realise, with her family history, that the dragon always destroyed the knight where she was concerned!

But she couldn't avoid seeing him until he gave her back the ring; she needed that back in her possession again before she spoke to Giles, had no leverage without the ring he so badly wanted returned.

Last night with Reece . . .

She sprang impatiently to her feet, needing to be away from this flat and sitting here was giving her the time to question exactly what had happened with Reece last night. The shop. There was always plenty to do there, especially after a busy week; she would go in and tidy up, dust the place down, and generally clean up the debris from the week.

Everything there looked so normal, untouched by the events of the last two days, that she quickly lost herself among the things she loved most in the world: her books. She had discovered long ago that she could lose herself among the covers of any book, that the reality of her own disordered world soon ceased to exist. Amanda had quickly realised that a book would hold Laurel enraptured for hours at a time, and had supplied her with an endless amount of them, particularly when she got older and was home from school. Laurel had known the books were a way of keeping her out of Amanda's way, but as she loved to read them she hadn't cared why they were given to her.

That love of books had followed her into adult life, had provided the ideal career for her when she received some money on her father's death eight years ago. She hadn't regretted the responsibility of her own shop one moment since she had made the decision.

It wasn't a big shop by any standards, but it was well fitted out, had a constant supply of popular books, her contacts in the business meaning she was able to order almost any book requested. She had acquired a loyal clientele the last few years, and she couldn't imagine doing anything else but running her bookshop. The fact that, if she didn't get her money returned she wouldn't have any choice, sent a shiver down her spine. She would stay here tonight, where she felt comfortable and at home. Besides, the thought of going back to her flat still made her nervous.

The leather sofa along one wall of her small office wasn't the most comfortable piece of furniture she had ever tried to sleep on, being too short, and very hard, the heating in the shop having gone off long ago too, the coat she had pulled over her providing her with little warmth. But she felt safe and unthreatened, her lids fluttering closed as she finally drifted into sleep.

'Where the hell have you been all night?'

Laurel's mouth quirked at Reece's impatient anger, easily discernible over the telephone when he called her at the shop the next morning. She had briefly returned to her flat earlier to shower and change her clothes, had ten minutes until opening time; Reece's telephone call certainly hadn't come as a surprise to her. After all, the romantic he assured her was in him would have checked that his new fiancée was well after the ordeal she had gone through yesterday.

'Reece, how nice of you to call so bright and early,' she returned lightly.

'It isn't "nice" at all,' he grated with controlled violence. 'Where have you been?'

Some knight he was turning out to be! 'Been, Reece?' she pretended ignorance.

His muttered expletives came clearly down the telephone. 'Stop acting so blasé, Laurel,' he rasped. 'I telephoned you several times last night——'

'I didn't receive any calls,' she denied in a puzzled voice.

'Of course you didn't, *you weren't there*!' he shouted impatiently.

'I wasn't?'

'*You know damn well*—— Laurel, where were you?' he demanded furiously.

'I haven't been anywhere, Reece,' she assured him distantly.

'Don't lie to me,' he snapped. 'When you didn't answer my calls I went around to your flat.'

'You did?' She was wary now.

'I banged on the door until one of your neighbours came out and told me it had to be damned obvious you weren't at home,' he gave an angry growl. 'I felt a damned fool.'

Laurel could believe that. It might even have been amusing to witness!

'Especially when the woman also informed me you had left over an hour ago and hadn't come back,' he continued relentlessly.

She bristled angrily. 'I wasn't aware my movements were being monitored by my neighbours! Maybe I should think of moving.' She frowned her displeasure with the idea that the people in the building where she had lived the past five years should know so much about her movements.

'You should think about telling me where you

were all night!' Reece bit out viciously. 'Did you go to Gilbraith?' he demanded furiously.

She drew in a choked breath, her hand trembling as she grasped the receiver. 'You *have* to know he's the last person I want to see right now!' she snapped bitterly.

'The last person?' Reece queried softly, suspicious of her vehemence.

Laurel frowned her irritation as she realised she had revealed more of her venom for Giles in that icy statement than she had meant to. 'He did jilt me,' she pointed out harshly.

'I thought it was only called that when you were left waiting at the church?'

'Our marriage plans were being arranged. We—I don't want to talk about Giles Gilbraith or any of the plans we made together,' she dismissed impatiently. 'I did not see him last night.'

'Then who did you see?' Reece questioned with icy intent.

'No one,' she answered bluntly. 'Now I have to open the shop——'

'I haven't finished talking to you yet——'

'We're meeting tonight at seven-thirty,' she reminded. 'We can talk about this then. If we must,' she muttered.

'Oh—we must,' he assured her grimly. 'This conversation is far from at an end.'

'Reece,' she spoke softly before he could slam the telephone down on her, as his aggression promised he would. 'Besides the fact that you're untidy and I'm not, you like to get up early and I don't, I think there's something else you should know about us.'

For a moment there was silence, then came a wary, 'Yes?'

'You have a lousy temper and I dislike being shouted at!' she bit out tautly. 'But there does appear to be one thing we do have in common,' she rasped rigidly. 'We both like the last word—and this time the victory is mine!' She slammed the phone down on him before he had a chance to say anything more, half expecting him to call straight back, surprised when he didn't; after all, they *did* both like the last word. The telephone remained silent.

The morning began busily and remained that way, Laurel breathlessly answering the telephone just after eleven o'clock, mechanically reciting the shop's number.

'Just remember, Laurel, I'm the one trying to help you!' Reece rasped before ringing off abruptly.

She stared at the receiver in outraged silence. *Helping* her! He called taking over her life, acting like a possessive fiancé, *helping* her? He *was* insane!

'Laurel,' Polly gained her attention as she stared off into space. 'This gentleman is calling about the book he ordered.'

She put down the telephone receiver in controlled movements, composing the smile of confidence on her lips before turning to face the customer, knowing that for Polly to have brought him over to her over a simple ordering of a book meant they had to be having trouble getting it. She was right, and it took several minutes to soothe the customer's ruffled indignation.

As soon as the man had gone she picked up the receiver, dialling with abruptly precise movements. 'Do something for me, Reece,' she rasped between gritted teeth as she recognised his voice. '*Don't* help me!' She slammed the receiver down for the second time that day, hoping the noise hurt his ears.

'I didn't think he was that angry,' Polly remarked ruefully.

Laurel spun around, her expression still fierce. 'Who?'

Her assistant frowned her puzzlement at Laurel's terseness. 'The man who just left . . .'

Her brow cleared as she made an effort to compose herself. 'He wasn't,' she assured the other woman calmly. 'Not once I'd explained the difficulty we're having.'

'Then why——' Polly shook her head, realising by Laurel's expression that the reason for her anger had nothing to do with the customer and that it was none of her business. 'Reece is certainly making his ownership known, isn't he?' she said with relish.

The dark scowl reappeared over her eyes. 'What?' she rasped.

'Your ring,' Polly looked at it admiringly. 'The girls are all agog with the size of the diamond,' she added by way of explanation. 'It must have cost a fortune. I——'

'I'm sure it did.' She thrust the hand wearing the ring into the pocket of her tailored skirt. 'But the size and impressiveness of the ring a man gives you doesn't mean he's as big!'

'I didn't mean——'

'I know you didn't,' she groaned self-disgustedly, angry with herself for taking out her frustration with Reece on poor innocent Polly; it was only natural to show interest in such a conspicuous ring. 'I'm just—a little tense,' she excused.

'Pre-wedding jitters,' Polly nodded understandingly. 'It is an awful time, isn't it?'

'Awful,' she agreed vehemently as she remembered how difficult Reece was now choosing to be.

'I should imagine Reece's sudden engagement has come as a bit of a shock to some people,' Polly mused.

She was suddenly tense. 'Oh?'

'At the bank,' Polly nodded. 'After all, bankers are supposed to be staid, lacking in impulsiveness.'

Why hadn't she thought of that? After announcing his engagement so suddenly Reece would look very stupid if it ended as suddenly! There might even be a woman in his life he was trying to fob off. No, that wasn't Reece's style at all; he would tell a woman if he no longer wanted her. But she could see now how he wouldn't want to look impulsively irresponsible twice in such a short length of time. But he should have trusted her with his dilemma instead of inventing all that nonsense about showing her the error of her ways!

'Thank you for the roses.'

Laurel turned to look at Reece, admiring the way his dinner jacket fitted his broad shoulders and tapered waist, the way his dark hair just brushed the snowy white collar of his plain silk shirt. He always dressed in taste and style, no one could dispute that.

He grinned across the table at her as they sat at the dinner table together. 'Although I thought I was supposed to be the romantic one,' he added with amusement.

One dark blonde brow arched. 'You don't like white roses?'

'I love them. But it certainly made the senior staff sit up and take notice when the young woman walked into my office with them!'

'Do you have any idea how difficult it was to get a florist to deliver on the same day this close to Christmas?' Laurel rebuked.

His hand covered hers as it rested on the table-top. 'I'm more interested in *why* you had them delivered,' he told her intently.

She shrugged. 'I didn't have the time to leave the shop and come myself.'

'Laurel!' he reproved.

She sighed, having regretted the impulse that had made her send the roses half a dozen times since making the call to the florists. 'I just realised that perhaps I haven't been completely fair to you,' she admitted grudgingly. 'After all, you *are* helping me out. It can't be easy for you being engaged to me.'

'Oh it isn't,' he agreed gravely, the twinkle in his eyes belying his serious tone.

'Reece, I'm being serious,' she admonished.

He sobered, frowning. 'I can see that you are. Would you mind telling me what isn't fair and can't be easy for me?'

'The predicament you put yourself in at the
bank when you announced our engagement to
save my humiliation.' And while she was grateful
to him, had sent the roses as an apology for her
unreasonable behaviour, she had to admit she had
also done it in a way that would appeal to his
sense of the ridiculous, the sending of the roses
having nothing to do with being a romantic; she
had guessed that he had never had a woman send
him flowers before.

Dark brows rose. 'Predicament?'

'A sudden engagement followed by an even
quicker ending of it could be very awkward for
you,' she explained impatiently.

His expression cleared. 'How and when I
choose my wife has nothing to do with anyone
but myself and her. It was nice of you to think of
me, Laurel,' he said lightly. 'But if you think I'm
continuing this engagement under my terms
because I fear any embarrassment to myself then
forget it; I told you, I want to be engaged to you.'

'You're really serious about it being a real one?'
she gasped disbelievingly.

'Yes. I've already sent the announcement to the
newspapers.'

'You've *what*?'

'I'm sure you heard what I said,' he derided.

'You had no right!'

'Of course I did.' He was unperturbed by her
unmistakable anger. 'I'm your fiancé.'

'Reece——'

'Another fault of mine I forgot to mention,' he
said pleasantly. 'I'm stubborn!'

'And I don't like having someone trying to

arrange my life for me.' She stood up in controlled movements.

'Where do you think you're going?' Reece's indulgent manner was gone, his tone steely.

She looked down at him scornfully. 'Home.'

He stood up too, throwing some money down on the table for their dinner as the waiter approached with their bill, one glance at Reece's face enough to stop him in his tracks. 'Not without me you aren't.' He helped Laurel on with her wrap. 'We're a couple now, Laurel.'

She was tight-lipped as they left the restaurant, snuggling down in the warmth of the Jaguar as Reece drove her home. 'Don't bother,' she told him as he would have got out of the car with her. 'You aren't coming in.' Flames gleamed in her eyes as she turned to look at him. 'At least, not with me. As for the roses, I hope they're the sort with huge thorns.' She got out of the car.

Reece uncoiled himself at a more leisurely pace, leaning on the roof of the car to watch her as she approached the building. 'I'll pick you up again at seven-thirty tomorrow night,' he drawled.

She stiffened in the act of opening the door, turning slowly. 'I don't seem to be making myself clear——'

'You're making yourself very clear.' He looked very dark and confident in the light given off from the street-lamps. 'But I'm still going to remain in your life until I've made you realise what a lucky escape you've had from Gilbraith and any other relationship like that one.'

Her mouth twisted. 'You could put me off marriage completely!'

He smiled. 'I won't do that,' he assured her before the door swung shut behind her.

He sounded so confident, was so determined. God, she *hated* the helpless feminine feelings he induced in her!

'Where is it, Laurel?'

Her hand shook as she made herself continue in the action of switching on the lights, before slowly turning to look at Giles. He was lounging in one of her armchairs in the sitting-room, looked as if he had been doing so for some time. Just looking at him made her feel nauseous as she relived his violation of her home, fear engulfing her as she took in the knowledge that he had done it again just by being in here. And she knew by the derision in his eyes that he could tell exactly how she felt.

She stiffened her shoulders, taking off her velvet wrap with controlled movements. 'I won't ask how you got in,' she finally spoke coldly. 'Because I'm sure it's the same way you got in two nights ago.'

'Two nights ago?' He looked at her enquiringly.

She gave him a disgusted look. 'Don't try and pretend it wasn't you that broke in here then.'

'You were burgled?' He feigned surprise.

The police seemed happy to think that was all it was, the jewellery that was missing evidence of the crime—but she certainly wasn't!

'No,' she snapped.

'You mean someone just broke in here for the fun of it?' he taunted.

She was more convinced than ever that it had been him that wrecked her home! 'That was part of it, I'm sure,' she glared at him. 'You do realise that Reece could have come up with me just now.' She dreaded to think what would have happened if he had!

'I checked out the window,' Giles shrugged.

'You . . . What are you doing?' she gasped as he made a lunge for her arm.

'Very nice,' he murmured as he looked down admiringly at the diamond ring she wore, arching mocking brows at her. 'Harrington really is serious about this engagement, then,' he derided.

Laurel snatched her arm away. 'Very serious,' she told him with satisfaction, knowing it was true, but not in the way Giles believed.

'Then you no longer need my ring,' he ground out.

She gave him a pitying glance. 'You know the conditions for its return.'

'And you know I don't have the money,' Giles snapped impatiently, standing up.

'I know you *had* it—just as I know you were the one who broke in here two days ago.' She looked at him accusingly. 'If you had taken the trouble to ask I could have told you the ring wasn't here,' she derided. 'As it isn't here now,' she added softly.

Fury glittered in his pale blue eyes. 'Then where the hell is it?'

She looked at him coldly. 'Where you can't touch it.'

He gave a scornful laugh. 'You're way out of your league, Laurel,' he warned softly. 'Give me the ring back and I'll just get out of your life.'

She shook her head. 'I can't do that.'

His eyes iced over. 'Would you like me to talk to Harrington about you?' he asked pleasantly.

Laurel stiffened. 'Concerning what?'

'The amount of nights I stayed here with you for one thing.'

They both knew he had never stayed anywhere with her, and after their night together so did Reece! She gave a tight smile. 'I somehow don't think he would believe you,' she drawled.

'Oh, I think he might be persuaded——' Giles broke off at her confident expression. 'My God,' he said slowly, wonderingly. 'He's had you himself, hasn't he?'

She winced at the crudity of the statement, nodding aloofly. 'Reece and I are lovers, yes,' she confirmed haughtily.

Giles gave a mocking laugh. 'And the two of you are still engaged?' he taunted.

Her head whipped back at the derision in his voice. Obviously he believed her incapable of a hot-blooded response to any man. She had thought so herself until her night with Reece! But he had brought out responses in her that were totally new and overwhelming.

'What's the matter, Giles?' she came back hardly. 'Can't you accept the fact that Reece is a better man than you'll ever be?'

'He's certainly a braver one!' he scorned. 'I'd be frightened of freezing to death in your arms!'

'Get out of here,' she said dully.

'Don't worry, I'm going.' He walked leisurely over to the door. 'I have a warm and willing wife waiting for me at home.'

'She's welcome to you!'

He smiled. 'Next time I come back you had better have the ring where you can get it,' he warned.

'Next time you come back use the doorbell,' she told him coldly.

'The single lock you put on your door while you're out isn't enough to keep me out,' he scoffed. 'And if I don't get the ring next time I may just decide to take that ice cube you're wearing in exchange; it looks as if it might be worth a few thousand.'

'Reece would find you if you did that,' she claimed confidently.

He paused at the open door. 'Considering how determined you are that he shouldn't know how stupid you've been I very much doubt that you would ever tell him you gave it to me!'

Laurel was shaking badly by the time he left. First Reece's bloody-mindedness, and now this! How much more could she take? And what was the point of it when all said and done? If Giles no longer had the money then he didn't have it, threats and warnings weren't going to make it suddenly appear. She was going to lose the only good thing left in her life, and she couldn't lift a finger to stop it. Unless . . . No, there was no way she could go to either Robert or Reece and ask them to lend her money. She hadn't asked anyone for anything in so long she didn't even think she would know how to go about it!

And she couldn't stay here for the night either. She changed into warm denims and a thick high-necked sweater the same blue as her eyes, packed some clothes for the morning in a small overnight case, knowing she wasn't going to be able to stay in this apartment again, intending to look for somewhere else to live as soon as she could.

The sofa seemed even more uncomfortable tonight, her problems going round and round in her head. She almost fell to the floor in fright as a knock sounded on the door. It was two o'clock in the morning, who could be knocking on a shop door that time of night? God, not another burglar! Burglars didn't knock, stupid, she chastised herself, staring apprehensively at the door as the handle was turned.

'I know you're in there, Laurel,' Reece's voice rasped through the glass. 'And you had better open this door before I really lose my temper!'

CHAPTER SIX

SHE could see him through the glass now as she approached the door, and what she saw didn't encourage her to open the lock. It had been snowing for some time now, everywhere gleaming white, and the black-clothed man looked all the more ominous against its brightness. Black cords moulded to his long legs, a black cable-knit sweater beneath the familiar black body-warmer, the only light in his harsh face the angry glitter of his golden eyes.

'Open the damned door, Laurel,' he ordered again, stamping his cold feet in the snow, rubbing his chilled hands together.

She clicked the lock, stepping back as he pushed his way inside.

'God, it isn't much warmer in here,' he glared. 'What the hell happened to the heating?'

Obviously being a 'morning man' didn't extend to the very early hours, Reece's mood terse and impatient. 'It goes off at night,' she shrugged dismissively.

He strode through to the office, looking down disgustedly at the blanket she had thrown back before getting off the couch. 'And you were going to sleep here,' he accused, sparks in his eyes.

'It isn't that bad——'

'The Antarctic is warmer!' he grated.

'Reece——'

'Is this where you were last night, too?' he demanded forcefully.

'If you will just calm down——'

'Calm down!' he repeated furiously. 'When I got home I telephoned your flat to see if you were all right, when I got no answer I thought, "she's sulking"——'

'I do not sulk,' she snapped.

'You sulk,' he stated flatly. 'So I tried again an hour later——'

'I could have been asleep!' she accused.

'Not in your own flat you couldn't,' he glared. 'Because you haven't been there the last two nights! Your neighbour told me, the same neighbour as last night,' he pointed out aggressively.

'Oh dear,' she grimaced.

'She certainly didn't take kindly to being woken up at almost two o'clock in the morning!' he snapped.

'Who would?'

'Indeed,' Reece bit out harshly. 'She told me you had left a couple of hours before with a man.' He watched her with narrowed eyes.

Her cheeks flamed bright red. 'That's a lie,' she instantly denied. 'I left alone. Good God, what does the woman do, stand with a glass against my wall?'

'I wouldn't know,' he dismissed curtly. 'I'm more interested in who the man was you didn't leave with.'

Laurel's gaze was suddenly evasive. 'There wasn't a man——'

'It was Gilbraith,' he instantly guessed. 'What did he want?'

She contemplated denying he had ever been there, but the mood Reece was in he was likely to turn violent if she tried to avoid answering him again. And he already looked as dark as the devil! 'His ring, of course,' she admitted with a sigh.

Golden eyes narrowed. 'Did you tell him I have it?'

'No,' she answered harshly.

'Why not?'

She moistened dry lips. 'I—I didn't want to involve you,' she said lamely.

'Not involve me!' he predictably scorned. 'You're wearing *my* ring now, Laurel, and I want Gilbraith out of your life once and for all.'

He wanted, did he! 'And what about what I want?' she demanded angrily.

'I'm going to take care of that, too,' he grated, thrusting her coat at her, taking a quick inventory of the room before striding over to pick up her overnight case. 'Is this all you have?' he rasped.

'Yes. But——'

'I-would-advise-you,' he spoke in a controlled voice, bundling her out of the shop and across the pavement to the silver Jaguar, 'not-to-say-anything-more.' He threw her case into the back of the car before pushing her into the passenger seat. 'Not unless you want to be made love to in the front seat of a Jaguar,' he threatened angrily as he climbed in beside her.

'I . . .' The glittering intent in his eyes as he turned to glare at her was enough to instantly silence her. He really meant it!

'You can talk now,' he told her harshly once he had thrown her suitcase down on the bed in his spare bedroom, looking at her challengingly, his chin thrust out determinedly.

How she wished she dare lash out and punch him on that chin, but somehow she had a feeling that the mood he was in he might react in kind—and she would definitely come out the worst in that encounter!

She looked at him steadily. 'You aren't sharing this bed with me tonight,' she told him abruptly.

He relaxed slightly. 'I'm not?' he drawled.

That helpless feeling was washing over her again! 'No,' she insisted aggressively.

'Fred missed you last night,' he told her huskily.

That piqued her. 'Only Fred?'

'I might have missed you—oh, a little bit, too,' he dismissed.

Her eyes darkened. 'Strange, I didn't miss either one of you,' she snapped.

'That's because you haven't spent enough time with us.' His good humour was returning, the dangerous glitter to his eyes fading. 'Yet,' he added softly.

Laurel could feel herself tensing. 'Reece——'

'Go and take a shower,' he cut in briskly. 'Otherwise you're likely to catch pneumonia. It was *freezing* in that shop!'

'Rubbish,' she dismissed, having been more accustomed to the cold there tonight. 'And I don't want to take a shower; I had one earlier.'

'Okay,' Reece shrugged. 'I'll just go and take one to warm up myself and then I'll be back.'

'You——'

'Yes?' he queried softly.

Colour darkened her cheeks at the unmistakable glint of desire in his eyes. 'I'm not going to sleep with you,' she told him raggedly.

'Neither of us is going to sleep tonight,' he assured her. 'You're my woman, and tonight you're going to realise that!'

She felt a shiver of apprehension run down her spine, her eyes dark with fear.

'Laurel, I'm not going to hurt you,' Reece chided gently. 'I thought I proved that the other night.'

He had also proved that she couldn't say no to him. And she knew that tonight was going to be no exception.

She unpacked her case while he was gone. There was no nightgown again, but she knew tonight she wasn't going to need one. She was already between the silken sheets when Reece came back into the room, her breath catching in her throat as he threw his robe aside and came to her. He was magnificent, beautifully sleek, like a fine sculpture.

She turned into his arms with an eagerness that shocked and dismayed her. Had she already become his sexual slave?

'You think too much, Laurel,' he murmured against her parted lips. 'And about the wrong things. This is what matters.' His thumb grazed her nipple and he felt her shudder in reaction. 'And this.' He claimed her lips. 'And this.' His hand curved about the warmth of her womanhood now, feeling her trembling increase.

'You and I are all that matters.' He took her mouth roughly.

Just a physical thing. Could she handle that? Could she *not* handle it? It was easier than trying to find the impossible, a man she could love, and as she didn't have the strength to fight this attraction towards Reece it would probably be more sensible if she just gave in to the feeling. It would be over soon enough, with no one hurt.

Tonight he wasn't asking for or giving gentleness, demanding, taking, inviting, inciting, until she pleaded for his possession, arching beneath him as she drove him deeper and deeper into the fathomless web of desire. The pinnacle climbed and reached they fell back to earth.

But Reece gave them no respite, kissing her, caressing her, taking them both back into that shower of sunlight time and time again, until amazingly it was morning, no time seeming to have passed at all.

Reece languorously caressed her breast as he cradled her against his shoulder. 'Now do I have to put a brand on you . . .?'

'I thought you already had,' she mocked, too deliciously tired to want to move, even though she knew she had to.

'I meant a visible one,' he teased.

She looked up at him with the knowledge of their effect on each other in her eyes. 'This isn't visible?'

He laughed softly. 'I wasn't sure if I would have to fight down your resistance all over again this morning; I'm glad I don't.'

She grimaced. 'I don't have the strength,' she told him truthfully.

'And you'll come back here tonight?' He frowned.

'Reece, I only stayed at the shop because I found the flat too oppressive after what had happened. It—I felt—uncomfortable there,' she understated.

His arms tightened about her understandingly. 'Move in with me,' he encouraged.

'I can't,' she told him simply. 'This is one thing, but actually moving in is something else. I like my independence too much.' And last night it had taken a serious beating!

'You want me to go grey before my time worrying about you?' he grimaced.

'I won't be living at the flat any more——'

'All the more reason to move in with me!'

She shook her head. 'I don't want to.' She could feel the way he flinched at her brutality, but she couldn't in all honesty take back the statement. Moving in with him was too—definite, allowed no freedom of choice in what was happening between them.

'Until you find somewhere else?' he pursued.

In the light of the fact that she had nowhere else to go just yet it would be churlish to refuse that offer, and as a compromise it wasn't a bad one. She readily accepted.

By the time she had been at the shop a couple of hours she had had time to regret her decision. She had never believed herself to be the type of woman to be taken in by charm and a blazing physical attraction. Although there had been no charm to Reece last night, and she had still gone to bed with him. She must be more like her mother than she had realised. God, it——

'Parcel, Laurel,' Polly interrupted her wanderings. 'It's marked "Personal".'

Laurel glared at the small, brown-paper wrapped package Polly had placed on her desk, having been taking a short break before she fell asleep on her feet. A personal parcel had to mean Reece, and ... Or did it? It couldn't be some other sick act on Giles's part, could it? She was reluctant to open it and see what lay inside—whichever man it had come from.

A key! What on earth ...! A frown marred her brow as she picked up the card lying in the lid of the small box, it read 'Please use it, Reece'. It was the key to his wing of the house!

'Okay?' Polly appeared in the doorway again.

She hastily placed the lid back on the box, pushing the card inside her bag. 'Fine,' she answered briskly. 'Are you busy out there?'

The other woman shook her head. 'It's gone surprisingly quiet.'

'Lull before the storm,' she predicted, knowing Christmas could be a strange time of year for business.

Polly frowned. 'You don't look well,' she sounded concerned. 'Are you coming down with something?'

Yes—it was called Reecitous! She had been thinking about him most of the morning, and the conclusions she had come to had all crumbled into the dust with the delivery of the key, knowing that it was meant to tell her she would

still have her freedom, that he made no ties on
her. And she would put a sure bet on him
knowing exactly what effect that would have on
her!

Living with a man she barely knew had more
problems than she had ever guessed, Reece's
untidiness something she gave up on after two
days of trying to pick up after him, his habit of
eating at irregular, and often very late, times,
something she found strange, too, not being a
nibbler herself. And then there was the way he
liked to bounce out of bed in the mornings while
she just wanted to snuggle down under the covers
and go back to sleep. He sang in the shower no
matter what time of night or day it was, was an
avid viewer of any and all quiz programmes on
the television. And he bought her flowers, and
chocolates, and cascaded her with compliments
about any and everything!

Laurel felt disorientated, tried to keep their
relationship to the physical arrangement they had
made when she had accepted his offer to stay here
for a few days until she found a new flat. But that
was a little difficult to do when he insisted on
treating her with all the consideration and care of
a new bride, telephoning her several times a day
just to talk to her, buying her gifts, always eager
to fall in with whatever plans she had for the
evening. And then there were the nights. Despite
her lack of experience in such relationships she
knew that no casual lover could ever talk to her
the way he did when they made love, could be so
concerned about her pleasure at all times, could

be so naturally intimate with her. All her preconceived ideas of what a relationship based purely on the physical should be were completely crushed by Reece as he wouldn't allow her to treat him in a detached and practical way. After only three days of living with him she was ready to admit she was totally confused. To herself, anyway. To Reece she remained outwardly cool—even when he insisted on walking about stark naked for hours at a time, often seeming to forget the need for clothes at all. He had no inhibitions, in bed or out of it, and to her surprise she was learning not to have any either.

She wasn't in love with him she was sure of that, confident in her decision not to allow herself to love any man. But physically . . .! Oh God, physically she couldn't refuse him. She looked on it as a sickness, and every sickness came to an end, one way or another. She *would* get over this weakness she had for Reece's kisses and caresses. She, Laurel Matthews, was not fatally ill, just a little sick.

'Laurel?'

She looked up at the man at her side, her head resting on his shoulder as they lay in bed together. She had arrived home half an hour ago to be met with a glass of the hot lemon tea she favoured after a hard day, the shower already running hot, her favourite lounging robe laid out on the bed. Only she hadn't got as far as putting on the robe yet. She had drunk the lemon tea, stepped into the shower, only to have Reece join her there, initiating the lovemaking that had ended in the bed they now relaxed in.

'What is it, darling?' he frowned. 'I've been talking to you the last few minutes,' he explained at her questioning look. 'You haven't heard a word I've said.'

She hadn't even been aware that he was talking! 'I'm sorry,' she was instantly contrite, her fingertips running lightly over his chest.

'Hectic day?' he sympathised.

It had been hectic, only two shopping days left until Christmas, people suddenly seeming to realise how close it was and panicking because they had nowhere near finished their shopping. It always seemed to be this way, and she could only hope to get through the next two days without collapsing from exhaustion. Sleepless nights and busy days just didn't mix!

'Very,' she nodded. 'I—What on earth was that?' She sat up in bed as a loud ringing noise filled the room.

'Dinner,' Reece said with satisfaction.

Her eyes widened. This wing of the house was completely self-sufficient, as Reece had claimed it was, a well-stocked kitchen in the lower floor. But they hadn't bothered to use it for any more than toast and coffee for breakfast, and it unnerved her to realise Reece had bothered to cook them dinner himself rather than have it sent from his father's kitchen as he usually did.

'What is it?' she asked warily.

'A sort of stew,' he announced confidently, as he left the bedroom. She hurriedly put on her robe and followed him to the dining area of the lounge.

He seemed to have thrown in a little bit of everything he could find in the least suitable from the kitchen cupboards, and though it was a little strange to come across strings of spaghetti, the overall taste was good. It was also a little too domesticated for her liking. They had spent the last few evenings alone through choice, although she felt sure their parents were aware of her car parked outside the last three nights, of the fact that dinner had been supplied for two rather than the usual one of those same three evenings. But spending the evenings alone and having what really amounted to room service was one thing, sharing a cosy dinner for two prepared by Reece put it all on a more intimate footing. And she didn't feel comfortable with it.

'You're wandering again,' Reece softly interrupted her thoughts. 'Tell me what's bothering you.' He reached across the table to take her hand in both of his.

'The spaghetti mainly,' she deliberately misunderstood him. 'It's a little disconcerting to be calmly eating and then suddenly have a string of it hit you on the chin!' She raised her napkin to the corner of her mouth where the sauce had once again escaped her. 'What made you put spaghetti in it anyway?'

'Well the recipe said baked beans.' He looked a little sheepish. 'And as I can't stand the things and won't have them in the house I decided that spaghetti would be a good replacement.'

'It's a—novel idea,' she said drily. 'Do you cook often?'

'You know I don't,' he drawled. 'I just . . .

tonight I just wanted to be alone with you, without any interruptions at all.'

She was instantly wary. 'Oh?'

He frowned. 'Laurel, when are you going to talk to me?'

'I thought I did.' Her surprise was genuine, having opened up more to him than she had really wanted, or expected to.

He sighed. 'Not about anything that's really important to you.'

She shrugged. 'There's only the shop——'

'Exactly,' he looked at her expectantly.

'What do you mean "exactly"?' Her eyes were narrowed as she released her hand from his, pushing her plate away, her appetite gone.

He drew in a ragged breath. 'You aren't going to tell me, are you?'

She retreated even further from him. 'Tell you what?' she avoided.

Reece stood up noisily, moving to the lounge area to pour them both a brandy. He put the brandy glasses down on the coffee-table, going to stand beside the fireplace, staring down brood-ingly into the flames the wood fire was giving out. He turned as she slowly followed him. 'Do you trust me, Laurel?' he prompted.

'In what context?' she returned guardedly.

His mouth twisted. 'Not as your lover,' he rasped. 'I'm well aware of the fact that I'm still only the man who surprises you out of your mind each time we make love by being able to tempt you into giving yourself to me!'

She winced at the pained accusation, although she could see the truth of it, suspected in her moments alone that Reece had put some sort of spell on her. In her more lucid moments she knew she had merely fallen prey to physical infatuation.

'In what way then?' she prompted coldly.

'As a friend, as someone who cares about you.' He watched her with narrowed eyes. 'Who would do his best to help you if he could.'

She turned away, unable to meet that fierce gaze. 'Reece, I don't . . .'

'Are you willing to lose it all for a little false pride?' he rasped.

Her stricken gaze returned to his face. 'What are you talking about?'

He shook his head, as if he couldn't believe the calm way she was behaving. 'I've tried to get you to talk to me,' he groaned. 'To open up. But you won't, and so——'

'Reece.' Her voice was slightly shrill now. '*What* are you talking about?'

He swallowed down the brandy. 'I've waited, I've given you every opportunity——'

'*Reece!*'

The glittering gold of his eyes as he glared at her was enough to tell her he was furiously angry with her. She knew his every mood now from those expressive eyes, the gold of anger, dismay, and physical arousal, the warm brown of pleasure, amusement, indulgence. He certainly wasn't physically aroused, but he *was* very angry and dismayed.

He marched over to the bureau in the corner of the room, impatiently flicking back the lid to take an envelope from one of the cubby-holes.

'This fell out of your handbag the other day.' He threw it down on the coffee-table between them. 'I've been waiting for you to talk to me about it.' He looked at her challengingly.

Laurel stared down at the envelope with it's distinctive business stamp at the top. She had searched everywhere for that letter the last few days, the possibility that Reece might have had it all the time not even occurring to her. 'It just "fell out" of my bag, did it?' she derided disbelievingly.

'Yes,' he bit out. 'You think I took it?' he accused harshly at her sceptical expression. 'Damn it, Laurel, you were the one that dropped your handbag in the bedroom the other day, spilling the contents all over the place.'

She remembered the occasion, the fluffy white rug at the foot of Reece's bed the scene of their lovemaking that evening, her bag getting knocked out of the way in the process. She had thought she had put everything back into it.

'It was under the bed,' Reece read her accusing thoughts. 'The maid handed it to me when I got home from work last night.'

'And you read it,' she scorned icily.

He ran a hand over his temple. 'I didn't mean to; I'm not into reading other people's mail. But I couldn't stop staring at it, kept getting the strangest feeling of foreboding, and——'

'Then you read it,' she snapped.

'Yes,' he confirmed irritably. 'What does it mean, Laurel? I thought you were doing well, so why haven't you paid your lease money for next year?'

Of all the things for Reece to have been given and read it had to be Campbells' letter explaining that her yearly lease money was very overdue!

It was still overdue, and likely to remain that way, Giles telephoning her only today to tell her he wouldn't even talk about the return of her money until she gave him his ring back. And as that was in Reece's possession she wasn't able to do that.

CHAPTER SEVEN

'FORGET I said that,' he sighed at the icy closed-in look in her eyes. 'I shouldn't have asked, it's none of my business. All I really wanted to do was offer to help you, to give you——'

'Money!' she cut in tautly. 'You want to give me *money*?'

Puzzlement flickered in his eyes at her vehemence. 'Laurel, I just want to help——'

'Then *don't* offer me money,' she rasped.

'But——'

'I'm not for sale, Reece,' she scorned contemptuously.

'*What did you say?*' The icy softness of his voice was a warning.

She braced her shoulders, facing him unflinchingly. 'You give money to your mistresses, I'm not your mistress. I go to bed with you because I've found I don't have too much choice about it.' She hated making the admission, but she had to make him understand exactly where he stood in her life. 'But I don't have to accept anything else from you.'

'No, you don't, do you,' he accepted disgustedly. 'Not even my company when we aren't in bed—so I'll take myself out for the rest of the evening!'

'It's your home,' she bit out. 'I'll leave. If it's what you want.'

'No—it isn't what I want,' he snapped. 'After all, we'll be going to bed together later!' He strode angrily from the room, the front door banging seconds later.

Laurel turned shakily, instinctively moving to the window, wincing as the Jaguar kicked up stones from the driveway as it was over-accelerated. She had never seen Reece that angry before—he had looked capable of strangling her before he left so abruptly.

But she didn't want the close intimacy he was trying to surround them with, wanted, as much as possible, to keep things impersonal between them. She had never realised how emotionally close you felt to someone once they became your lover. And after avoiding emotion in her life for fifteen years she didn't want it intruding into her life now. But she did want Reece in her life, needed to feel his arms about her in the night, to know the possession that never failed to make her peak in sexual pleasure.

So what did that make her? What sort of woman was she who required a man to make love to her every night but leave her completely alone at all other times? Obviously the sort of woman Reece had decided he could no longer tolerate!

'I did knock, but you didn't seem to hear me,' Amanda spoke lightly from the doorway.

She turned sharply, instantly on her guard. 'Yes?' she prompted abruptly.

'Everything all right, love?'

Amanda and Robert had seen the way Reece left and knew they had argued! 'Everything is fine,' she dismissed coolly. 'Reece—had to go out, that's all.' The steadiness of her gaze dared her mother to doubt that or to probe further.

Amanda came fully into the room. 'Robert and I wondered if the two of you would like to dine with us tomorrow evening,' she invited warmly.

They wanted to check that their offspring were getting along okay! 'I'll have to ask Reece, of course,' she answered smoothly. 'But I'm sure it will be all right with him.'

'Good,' her mother smiled her satisfaction. 'We really should all sit down together and try to sort out the arrangements for the wedding.'

'There's no rush,' she bit out tautly.

'Well, of course there isn't, darling,' Amanda agreed smoothly. 'But as you're already living here . . .'

Her cheeks blushed fiery red. She had persuaded Reece not to mention the break-in at her flat to their parents, insisting there was no point in worrying them. Obviously Amanda and Robert had drawn their own conclusions about their living arrangements when no explanation had been forthcoming! 'If you or Robert have any objections,' she began tightly.

'Of course we haven't, Laurel,' her mother instantly denied. 'Good heavens, neither of you are children for us to preach morals to. However,' she added firmly, 'there really doesn't seem to be any point in your waiting now. I'm sure you're both too sensible to make any silly mistakes, but even so . . .'

She nodded curtly. 'I'll tell Reece about your dinner invitation,' she said stiltedly. 'I'm sure he will want to come,' she effectively made known her own reluctance.

Her mother frowned. 'Darling, I know we've had our differences in the past, but are you sure everything is all right between you and Reece? You seem very tense. You can talk to me, you know,' she encouraged.

She would have laughed if it wouldn't genuinely have surprised her mother that she should be so bitter about the past. Amanda had selfishly lived her life the way she wanted, caring nothing for the happiness of the child she carried along in her wake. She could no more talk to Amanda, about anything, than she could fall in love, knowing it had been her mother's search for that elusive perfect love that had given Laurel all of her own unhappiness.

'There's nothing to talk about,' she shrugged dismissively. 'Now if you will excuse me, I have some accounts to do.' Things had been so hectic at the shop today, clearing away so late, that she had brought her books home with her. Now that Reece was aware of the problem she was having paying her lease she would have to take great care in locking the books away in her briefcase tonight. 'And I shouldn't worry about our living arrangements——'

'Laurel, we aren't worried,' Amanda protested. 'I'm just excited at the prospect of helping you with the wedding arrangements.'

She stiffened. 'I think you're being a little premature.'

Her mother looked surprised. 'Reece gave me the impression that he doesn't approve of long engagements.'

'When?' she demanded icily.

Amanda blinked. 'I—Well—Maybe I got the wrong idea,' she shrugged lightly.

She was sure her mother had taken a generalisation on Reece's part and applied it specifically to them. For all of the physical attraction between them Reece had agreed with her that the relationship would end one day. 'I'm sure you did.' She gave a cool inclination of her head. 'Is seven-thirty all right for tomorrow?' she deliberately put an end to the conversation.

Her mother looked disappointed. 'Seven-thirty will be lovely,' she nodded, leaving, as there seemed nothing else to say.

As far as Laurel was concerned she and Amanda had never had anything to say to each other, and she cursed the feelings of guilt that attacked her once her mother had left. Amanda had made her life, without thought for anyone but herself; it was too late for feelings of remorse or forgiveness.

She had done her cash books, tidied away from dinner, and was sitting up in bed reading a book when she heard Reece's car outside. She made no effort to pretend to be asleep as he came into the bedroom.

'The two of you look comfortable,' he remarked softly.

She glanced down indulgently at the bear that lay next to her in the bed, Fred's coat cleaner and glossier from the gentle wash she had given him, his ear and nose sewn on securely, the stitching of his mouth replaced. She usually sat him on the dressing table at night, although he lay between the pillows during the day. She had become fond of the tattered bear, she, who never became attached to anything.

She turned back to Reece; he looked tired as he sat down in the bedroom chair to slip off his shoes and straightened to pull off his tie. She wondered where he had spent the evening, but once again pride wouldn't let her show any sign of weakness in curiosity.

'Would you like some coffee?' she offered distantly.

'No, I . . .' His gaze clashed with hers. 'Yes,' he slowly changed his mind, 'I think I would.'

She climbed out of bed, wearing one of the new nightgowns she had purchased, all of her more intimate clothing replaced since Giles had broken into her flat and touched them all. She didn't bother with her slippers or the robe that matched the gown, neither necessary in the fully carpeted, centrally heated home.

Reece followed her as she padded down to the kitchen, her movements sure and quick as she made the coffee, all the time aware of a brooding gold gaze on her.

'It was the meal that started it, wasn't it?' he finally burst out.

She gave him a surprised look. 'It wasn't that bad.'

He gave the ghost of a smile at her attempt of humour. 'I'm talking about the existence of it, not its culinary worth.'

'We have to eat.' She shrugged, carrying the

tray of coffee back up to the bedroom as he would have taken it from her.

'In a restaurant, or meals cooked by other people,' he acknowledged, just behind her. 'But when I cooked the meal it was just too domesticated.'

'Is that what it was?' She deliberately kept her mood light. 'I thought it was a stew.'

'Laurel——'

'Cream and sugar?' she asked briskly.

Reece scowled. 'You know I don't take either!'

She gave another shrug, handing him a steaming cup of black, unsweetened coffee. 'Careful,' she warned. 'It will be hot.'

'I know that! Look, Laurel——'

'Yes?' She sat down on the side of the bed to drink her own coffee, crossing one knee over the other, knowing that the pale lilac gown suited her colouring perfectly. If Reece had expected to come home to an emotionally wrought woman he was disappointed!

His expression softened as he looked down at her. 'We have to talk,' he told her softly.

'That seems to be everyone's interest this evening.' Her voice was brittle.

His gaze sharpened with interest. 'Who else has been here tonight?' he asked suspiciously.

'Not Giles, if that's what you're thinking,' she rasped. 'I wouldn't invite him into your home.'

He relaxed slightly. 'Then who?'

'Amanda,' she told him flatly. 'She and your father want us to go over for dinner tomorrow.'

He nodded. 'And what else did she want to talk about?' he probed.

'Our living arrangements. The wedding,' she announced airily. 'Like when it's going to be!'

Reece's mouth tightened. 'And what about our "living arrangements"?' he grated.

'Although Amanda denied it, I think she and your father are a little—worried, about them.'

'Why?'

'You'll have to ask them.' She replaced her cup on the tray. 'I'm going back to bed now,' she informed him distantly. 'Good night.'

'Laurel, we haven't finished talking,' he protested impatiently.

'We don't have anything else to say.' She punched the pillow to make it more comfortable. 'Unless you want to apologise for your behaviour earlier?' She arched blonde brows at him.

'Apologise?' he repeated furiously. 'You're the one that's using me, damn it!'

Her eyes frosted over. 'Would you mind sleeping in your own room tonight?' she requested with chilly calm. 'I'll move my things out tomorrow.'

'You aren't leaving me just because I've taken exception to being used,' he warned.

'I thought what we were doing was mutually using each other,' she said icily.

'You know it's more to me than that.' He shook his head.

'You wanted me, Reece,' she sighed. 'And now you've had me. I have no intention of there ever being any more between us than that.'

'But I have,' His voice was dangerously soft. 'I made the engagement a real one, I can just as easily make it into a marriage.'

Her mouth twisted. 'Not unless you intend to carry me kicking and screaming into church!'

'No,' he sighed wearily. 'I don't intend doing that. Laurel, I only offered to help you earlier, you didn't have to react the way that you did,' he reasoned.

'I am not about to accept monetary help from the man who is my lover!' Her hands clutched the covers tightly to her.

Reece's eyes softened at the description. 'I just wanted to take that worried look out of your eyes,' he explained softly. 'I didn't intend any insult behind the offer.'

'Well, I took one,' she said adamantly. 'I am perfectly capable of taking care of myself—and my business.'

'Darling, I don't want to argue with you again,' he grimaced, as that seemed to be what they were about to do. 'I've just spent a miserable evening propping up a bar wondering where I went wrong, wondering whether or not you were going to be here when I got back, and if you were whether or not you would refuse to talk to me or just hit me over the head with the stew-pot!'

Relief flooded through her as he revealed where he had been all evening. She had thought . . . she had wondered if—God, she hadn't dared to think how she would feel if he had revealed he had spent the evening with another woman! And she deliberately didn't dwell on it now.

'As you can see,' she replied in a controlled voice, 'I am here. I am talking to you. And I don't have the stew-pot in my hand. However, I do want you to sleep in your own room tonight, and I will be moving out tomorrow.'

'Where?'

'I haven't found another flat yet.' To be truthful she had forgotten to look for one! 'But I can always move into a hotel until I have.'

'No,' Reece stated firmly.

Her eyes widened. 'What do you mean, no?'

'Christmas is in two days time, and I have no intention of letting you spend it in a *hotel*!'

'You——'

'Please don't lose your temper with me again,' he cut in pleadingly. 'I'll accept that you no longer want me to sleep with you, I'll even go back to my own bedroom like a good little boy,' he grimaced. 'But I want you to spend Christmas here. With me.'

She didn't really want to go to a hotel either. But she didn't know if she could stay here, either.

'I won't try to pry again,' Reece sensed her weakening. 'But if you do need someone to talk to I'll be here.'

She chewed on her bottom lip, tempted, and yet not altogether trusting his easy acceptance of the termination of their sleeping together. But he looked earnest enough, and because she really didn't want to spend the holiday in a hotel she decided she was just *too* suspicious. Reece was a gentleman, he wouldn't try and force himself on her. 'If you're sure that arrangement can work out,' she agreed hesitantly.

'Laurel, I'm not going to come creeping back in here when you're asleep,' he chided her reluctance. 'I do have some control.'

If he did she hadn't seen any evidence of it the last few days—and nights. It seemed the merest glance could induce Reece to carry her off to bed, and she couldn't help wondering if he would be able to keep his promise.

It hadn't occurred to her that she would be the one who would find it difficult! But after two hours of turning about miserably in the bed trying to get comfortable she had to accept that she missed their making love, missed falling asleep in Reece's arms. And she had a feeling Reece had known exactly how she would feel! But if he expected *her* to be 'creeping into *his* bed while he was asleep' he was in for a disappointment. In fact she was grateful to him for showing her how dependent she was becoming on him, hadn't realised just how deeply she was becoming involved. She fell asleep safe in the knowledge that she had ended the affair before she became too enmeshed to escape.

Reece didn't look as if he had slept at all the next morning, his eyes dark, his face pale, having no appetite for the toast and coffee she had prepared for him, giving her a terse goodbye before leaving for work.

He looked even worse by the time they joined their parents for dinner, and his mood was volcanic, ready to erupt at the least provocation. That provocation came from an unexpected quarter!

He had scowled and glowered at Amanda and Robert as they constantly touched and smiled at each other during dinner, and he sat in brooding silence as they all drank their coffee in the lounge afterwards. Laurel would probably have found his mood funny if she weren't feeling so tense herself! If this was sexual tension then she had been better off before she experienced lovemaking or the terrible withdrawal symptoms!

'Laurel,' Amanda spoke lightly. 'I know you said you didn't want to discuss the wedding, but there is one thing I would like to say about it.'

She had stiffened warily, and she could see Reece's mouth had tightened when she glanced at him. 'Yes?' she prompted.

'Don't you think it would be nice if Dan could come?'

The question, after years of not even mentioning Dan's name, came as something of a shock to Laurel, and she stared at her mother as if she had never seen her before. Then she turned quickly to look at Reece, the furious glitter in his eyes telling her he didn't appreciate Amanda's mention of Dan either!

'Dan?' she guardedly repeated.

'Yes,' Amanda went on determinedly, not immune to the sudden tension in the room, but seeming intent on saying what she wanted to anyway. 'The letter he put in with his Christmas card said he had some holiday time coming up in February, and that he had thought of spending it in England.'

Laurel swallowed hard. 'Dan *wrote*—to you?' She didn't even try to hide her incomperehension at him doing such a thing.

A shadow passed over her mother's eyes. 'He's always written to me, Laurel,' she said softly. 'Just as I've always written back.'

She couldn't believe it. Dan, her darling Dan,

writing to the woman who had destroyed them, who had ripped them apart. It couldn't be true!

CHAPTER EIGHT

'I WANT to know how Dan figures in your life.'
Reece demanded as soon as they were alone, back
in his wing of the house now.

Laurel felt so weary and let down she could
hardly walk. She had managed to gloss over the
awkwardness of the conversation about Dan by a
non-committal answer, but had been grateful
when Robert changed the subject completely,
leaving her to her confusion and Reece to his
brooding anger.

She was still trying to take in the fact that her
mother and Dan had kept in touch all these years.
She hadn't believed such a thing possible, but
how else could Amanda know of his plans to have
a holiday over here?

'Laurel.' Reece was more in control now as he
poured them both a drink, had refused a brandy
at his father's only a few minutes earlier, in his
impatience to leave. 'I want to know exactly what
this Dan means to you.' He faced her across the
room as she sipped at the reviving alcohol.

Dan. Dan, with the wavy black hair and
laughing blue eyes. Dan, whom she had always
worshipped.

'Who the hell is he that my father calmly sat
there and took Amanda's interest in him?' he
continued harshly. 'The *love* in her voice when
she spoke his name?' he added disgustedly.

Laurel chose to ignore the latter, although she knew it was true, had heard that same emotion in her mother's voice as she talked of Dan. But that Robert knew all about Dan she didn't doubt; how else could there have been compassion rather than anger in his eyes as he looked at his wife?

'If *my* wife had spoken of another man in that same way I would have killed him—and then her,' he grated.

The savage couldn't be denied in him now, and Laurel looked at him unflinchingly. 'Would you expect your father to be jealous of you?' she murmured.

His eyes widened. 'Of course not. What sort of question is that?'

She shrugged, tired beyond imagining, not understanding the way Dan had kept in touch with her mother and not with her. 'A valid one,' she said flatly.

'Valid? But——' His eyes narrowed now. 'Who is he, Laurel?' he asked in a hushed voice.

She drew in a ragged breath. 'When my mother and father got married it was his second marriage . . .'

'He had a son from his previous marriage?' Reece realised in a strangulated voice.

She nodded wordlessly. For eleven years Dan had been her adored older brother, not seeming to mind when she tagged along with him and his friends when they went out, that he was often expected to baby-sit for her when he got older. And then had come the divorce. Laurel hadn't been able to believe it when her parents told her she was to stay with her mother and Dan was to go with his father. A brother and sister couldn't be parted in that cruel way, she had screamed at them. But Dan wasn't really her brother, only her half-brother, and the law said he had to go to his father. She had pleaded and begged to go with them but it had got her nowhere, and when her father moved to America a year later he had taken Dan with him, severing all contact between them except the letters that had become stilted and finally stopped altogether. Laurel had run away from her mother half a dozen times after that and had to be brought back each time; hating her mother so much she could barely speak to her. And she still hated her.

'Dan is your brother,' Reece said incredulously.

'Half-brother,' she corrected bitterly. 'That distinction made all the difference at the divorce.'

He swallowed hard, refilling her glass with brandy as she held it between numb fingers. 'He went with your father?'

'Of course he went with my father,' she snapped, glaring at him.

'Darling——'

'Don't!' She stood up, avoiding his hands as he would have reached for her. 'I don't like to be touched!' she spat out.

Reece became suddenly still, his eyes deeply golden. 'Laurel, Amanda had no claim on him——'

'She didn't want him anyway,' her voice rose heatedly. 'Just as she didn't want me!'

He shook his head. 'If that were true the court could easily have given you to your father.'

'Keeping me was a way of getting back at him for their failed marriage,' Laurel insisted.

'You don't know that——'

'I know that she never once cuddled me or told me she loved me after Daddy and Dan left, that she kept moving me from home to home, that somehow it was always my toys that got "lost" in those moves. I know that she was relieved when Daddy and Dan went to America so that I couldn't see them any more.' Her voice broke emotionally, never having forgotten how her mother had said 'it's for the best', when Laurel had told her of her father's transfer.

'Then why did Dan keep in touch with her?' Reece reasoned.

She didn't know, felt betrayed by the act. How could he have so easily forgiven Amanda for what she had done to them!

'Laurel,' Reece spoke softly as he saw the anguish on her face. 'You were a child at the time, you don't know exactly what happened.'

'I know my mother has never cared for anyone or anything else but herself——'

'She loves you——'

'No,' she scorned. 'Parting me from my father and Dan was not an act of love!'

'You don't know all the details——'

'I don't need to,' she snapped. 'And if Amanda thinks she can make everything right by inviting Dan to our wedding then she's mistaken!'

'Is there going to be a wedding?' he prompted huskily.

She turned blazing violet eyes on him. 'You know there isn't!' she dismissed impatiently.

'It might be nice if Dan gave you away,' he suggested softly.

'I said no, Reece,' she grated.

'Of course February is a long way off——'

'I won't change my mind,' she said firmly.

'No, I meant it might be too far,' Reece frowned. 'I'm not sure I can wait six or seven weeks to make you my wife.'

'You would have to wait six or seven *lifetimes* for me to marry you!' She put her glass down with a solid thud. 'You were right, Reece, being engaged to you has shown me how wrong I was to think I could be content with the sort of marriage I would have known with Giles, how wrong I was to think I could be content with marriage to *any* man,' she added hardly. 'I realise now I don't want to be married to anyone.'

'Laurel——'

'It's been a long day, Reece,' she told him flatly. 'I think I would like to go to bed now.'

'Laurel, I won't let you do this,' he warned as she walked out of the room.

She knew once and for all that she was destined to live her life alone. Living with a man, with all the intimacy that implied, was not for her. She didn't want to rely on anyone, to have her inner feelings probed and analysed. And after the physical perfection she had known with Reece she didn't want any other man that way, either.

She took off Reece's ring once she got to her bedroom, laid it down in the dressing table, waited for the world to collapse and the sky to fall in. Nothing happened.

It was over, the madness with Reece was finally over.

'Where are you going with that suitcase?'

Laurel looked up slowly. She had wanted to leave quietly, without any fuss or argument, but she knew as she looked at the fury in Reece's face that wasn't going to be possible. 'I think that's obvious, don't you?' she replied calmly.

He was dressed for work in one of the formal three-piece suits that could make him into a stranger from the insatiable lover of the night. He looked as if his night had once again been sleepless, and Laurel was grateful for the make-up that camouflaged her own shadows.

'It's Christmas Eve,' he protested.

'So?' she shrugged.

'You can't go to a hotel on Christmas Eve!'

She knew that if Reece had his way he wouldn't let her go at all, and that was the reason she knew she couldn't stay. Reece had stopped playing games, and the emotion in his eyes frightened her.

'A hotel is exactly what I need,' she told him cruelly. 'The lack of intrusion, and the formality, are exactly what I want.'

He flinched, a pulse beating at the side of his mouth. 'Don't do this to me, Laurel.'

Her hand tightened on the handle of her suitcase. 'You're a grown man, Reece, you knew my feelings concerning our relationship, and you walked into it with your eyes open.'

'Because I'm not a coward,' he rasped.

Her mouth twisted. 'Neither am I,' she drawled. 'I'm just a realist.'

'You're hard, and . . . Where's your ring?' He frowned down at her bare left hand.

'I left it in the bedroom,' she told him flatly.

'Our engagement——'

'Is at an end,' she bit out tautly. 'Don't worry, I'll tell everyone that you were the one to realise you had made a mistake,' she taunted, knowing this last was an injustice to him. And yet she made no apology for saying it; it was exactly what she intended telling people if they asked.

'I don't want you to go, Laurel——'

'I know,' she accepted gruffly. 'Despite it all, all that you know I am, and can never be, you still want me.' She had seen the emotion in his eyes last night, just as she could see it in his eyes now. 'You've become too involved, Reece, can't you see that?' she reasoned. 'From being a caring and helpful stepbrother you've taken on the possessiveness of——'

'A husband?' he finished harshly. 'Maybe that's because it's what I always wanted to be to you, from the moment I first saw you.'

This was what she had hoped to avoid by leaving without seeing him! 'Reece, please don't——'

'I looked at you and I wanted you,' he continued remorselessly. 'But as soon as Amanda began seeing my father you treated me as if I had the plague. And because you had already gone through the trauma of your mother's two broken marriages I decided to give you time to get used

to this third family. But you never changed. Each
time we had a family dinner I expected you to
have mellowed, but you never did, treated me as
frostily as you did our parents. When your
mother received that invitation to your engagement party it was like a fist between my
eyes,' he recalled raggedly.

'Please, Reece,' she trembled. 'I don't want to
hear any of this.'

'Why not?' His eyes were unusually bright.
'Because it makes *you* responsible for someone
else's emotions for a change?' he rasped. 'You *are*
responsible, Laurel, you're responsible for my
loving you, for my wanting you, for my not being
able to live without you.'

She swallowed hard. 'You'll live,' she assured
him shakily.

'No, I won't,' he told her flatly.

Her gaze searched his face desperately, frantically looking for something that would tell her
he didn't mean it, that he was just trying to
frighten her. He was shockingly serious.

'This is blackmail, Reece,' she shook her head.
'And I won't be blackmailed.'

His mouth twisted. 'I'm not talking about
suicide, Laurel, I'm talking about the inner me,'
he bit out. 'The me that loves you——'

'You *don't* love me!' she snapped.

'Oh yes, I do,' he nodded, sighing heavily.
'And for a few days you were mine.'

'You'll get over it——'

His scornful laugh interrupted her. 'I won't do
that, either. But if it makes you feel better to
believe that then do so.' He turned away, his back

rigid with control. 'But while you're living that cold and lonely life you have mapped out for yourself I want you to know that I love you, that I've loved you for the past year, and that I'll go on loving you. The fact that you refuse to let yourself love me in return isn't going to change that, nothing will change that. So I wish you happiness in the life you've chosen for yourself,' he rasped.

It was a hollow wish after what he had just said, and Laurel didn't stay to dispute it, letting herself out of the house, having left him the key to the door with her ring on the dressing table, the lock clicking shut with finality behind her.

CHAPTER NINE

LOVE. She had known Reece loved her even before he said the words, had guessed—and that had been the reason she was running away. The love of a man like Reece would consume, devour, and she had already lost too much to the emotion, she daren't risk any more.

Reece was a braver person than she, wasn't afraid to give his love even though he knew it wasn't returned or wanted. She had relentlessly ignored the love in his eyes these last few days, had chosen to believe he wanted the brief relationship that she did, but finally she had known she couldn't pretend any more, Reece no longer willing to accept the casual relationship between them that was all she would ever want. She had known when he stormed out of the house after their argument the other evening that he loved her, had seen the pain in his eyes as he flung those bitter words at her. But she had forced that knowledge from her mind when he asked her to stay on in separate bedrooms, hadn't wanted to admit it. But this morning she had once again seen that love, and known Reece no longer intended to hide what he felt for her, no matter what pressure it put on her or how hurt he got in the process.

And she had hurt him, could do no other when she didn't love him in return.

He was a good man, a kind man, and she knew that at the moment he loved her beyond reason, that he had stooped to any subterfuge to get her to accept him in the relationship he really wanted, that he had announced their own engagement at her party in the hopes of eventually persuading her to make it a real one, that he was now willing to risk his pride to let her know of his love and encourage her to love him.

She couldn't.

'Telephone call for you, Laurel.' Polly looked into the staff-room where Laurel was supposed to be taking her morning coffee-break; in reality she had been staring off into space.

Her startled gaze flew to her assistant. 'Who . . .?'

'Your mother,' Polly told her ruefully.

She moistened suddenly dry lips, following the other woman down to her office. 'Er—did she say what she wanted?'

'No,' Polly shrugged. 'Just that she wanted to talk to you.'

Dan. It had to be about Dan. God, she hoped she was ready for this!

'Yes?' Her voice was unnaturally sharp as she acknowledged her mother's call.

'Shall we meet for lunch?' her mother returned without preamble.

She drew in a ragged breath. 'I can't, I'm afraid,' she refused with genuine regret. 'I've just taken the only break I'll be having today.' And she had only taken that one because she felt close to collapsing, not even having had a cup of coffee this morning after her sleepless night. 'It isn't that I don't want to meet you,' she hastened to explain. 'We're just very busy.' She had intended calling her mother herself later to arrange a meeting, had known it was inevitable.

'You do realise we have to talk?' her mother probed.

'Oh yes,' she agreed with feeling.

'I mean really talk, Laurel,' she spoke firmly.

'Yes,' she acknowledged hardly.

'How about this evening?' her mother suggested. 'Before you and Reece have dinner? I could come over, and——'

'I won't be at Reece's tonight,' she interrupted sharply. 'Perhaps I could drive over and see you?'

'Well, of course, Laurel.' Her mother's puzzlement was evident in her voice. 'Look, if you and Reece are dining in town tonight we could——'

'Reece and I aren't eating in town tonight,' she cut in coolly. 'We aren't having dinner at all. At least, not together,' she added brittlely.

'You've argued?' Amanda realised in dismay.

'We've realised we aren't suited after all,' she corrected. 'We have nothing in common——'

'But you love each other——'

'No,' she denied harshly.

'Reece loves you,' her mother insisted.

God, did he go around telling everyone! No, she wasn't being fair to him; Reece wasn't the sort of man who would publicly proclaim his love to all and sundry. But if she had seen his love for her why shouldn't other people see it, too?

'You would have to discuss Reece's feelings with him,' she said stiffly. 'But I am not in love with him. Our engagement is at an end.'

'I'm so sorry,' Amanda's regret sounded genuine. 'There's no hope of——'

'No,' she dismissed abruptly.

'I see,' Amanda sighed. 'In that case Robert and I would like you to spend Christmas with us.'

'I—That isn't necessary.' Her suitcase in the corner of the room was evidence of the fact that she hadn't yet booked into a hotel, but she hadn't spent Christmas with her mother in years, and she had no intention of spending this one with her, either.

'I'd really like it if you would, Laurel,' Amanda encouraged.

She wasn't exactly pleading, but it was there in her tone of voice none the less. And Laurel didn't like the guilt it made her feel. Her mother had made her choices, had sacrificed the happiness of her child for what she wanted, why should Laurel feel in the least guilty about making *her* own choices.

'I have other plans,' she dismissed coldly.

'Oh ...' Amanda gave a disappointed sigh. 'Dinner, then. Surely that isn't asking too much?'

Was it? She didn't know. As long as she didn't have to see Reece, perhaps not. 'Will Reece be there?'

'Well, I haven't invited him, but I can't answer for his father,' Amanda answered honestly. 'But the two of us have to talk and I don't think it should wait until after Christmas.'

Considering the fact, Laurel thought bitterly, that it had taken Amanda fifteen years to get around to this talk she didn't think another few days would make much difference. But she didn't want to wait either, and although she didn't relish the thought of possibly running into Reece again just yet she knew she would have to see him some time, that their family ties dictated she must.

'Dinner tonight will be fine,' she accepted stiltedly. 'Although for everyone's sake I would like you to call me if Reece definitely is going to be there; it could only be embarrassingly awkward for us all.'

'Laurel——'

'Yes?' she prompted hardly as her mother broke off hesitantly.

'Laurel, I—I——'

She could feel the same sense of panic she had known with Reece this morning, her palms becoming clammy.

'I love you, Laurel,' her mother told her softly before ringing off.

Pain ripped across her chest, pain such as she had never known before. *Amanda* loved her? She *wouldn't* believe that! Because if she did it made a mockery of the decisions she had made concerning her own life, and it was those decisions that kept her away from the pain of loving.

The pain in her chest continued.

'I realise I'm probably the last person you want to see,' Reece spoke softly. 'But I have somethings I have to talk to you about.'

She had stiffened at the sound of his voice, looking up slowly from her sitting position at her desk, the day over, only Polly left in the shop now as she tidied away the books left out on the counter; she must have let Reece in.

He looked even more tired than he had this morning, and Laurel knew she was to blame for that. She didn't flinch, looking at him steadily.

'I have something to give you, too,' he added huskily.

Her mouth twisted. 'Isn't exchanging Christmas gifts a little inappropriate now?'

He shook his head. 'This isn't strictly a Christmas gift.'

'Oh?' She was wary, turning briefly to Polly as she stood behind Reece.

'Have a good Christmas,' her friend told her. 'You too, Reece.'

'Thank you.' The smile he gave didn't quite reach his eyes.

Laurel walked past him to go to the door with Polly, the two of them having exchanged gifts earlier in the day. Her expression was pensive as she came back into the office, not having expected Reece to just come to the shop and see her like this.

She made no effort to sit down, eyeing him questioningly as he sat on the side of her desk. 'What can I do for you?'

He gave a rueful smile. 'Make the sun come out in the middle of winter, the flowers bloom, the——'

'Reece!' she snapped.

'Sorry,' he said without regret. 'I forgot you don't like to hear things like that.'

'You didn't forget,' she said dully, knowing he was hitting out at her because she had hurt him.

'No,' he acknowledged tautly. 'I hoped you might have felt differently since this morning.'

She looked at him guardedly. 'Why should I have done that?'

He shrugged. 'Because you know I love you, and because you don't really like hurting people.'

She had wondered if he had spoken to her mother, but his explanation told her he hadn't. 'Why are you here?' she prompted again.

'To give you this.' He reached into his breast pocket and pulled out an envelope. 'And before you look at it I want you to know that there's nothing you can do to stop it now.' He held out the envelope to her.

Inside she found a receipt, from Campbells, for the exact amount of her lease, and it was made out to her.

'I——'

'Another thing you should know is that I don't want the money back.' He held her gaze remorselessly.

Her mouth opened and closed without a sound coming out. He had calmly paid her lease for the next year and now he claimed he didn't want reimbursement!

She had spent most of the day in a fog of misery, wondering how much longer she would be allowed to stay open. And now this. For all that she had said about not taking money from him she was tempted to accept this *fait accompli*. But she couldn't; she paid her own way in life or not at all.

'You can hardly accuse me of trying to buy you when we're no longer together,' he added tautly. 'I did it because I wanted to, Laurel,' he told her softly. 'Not for any ulterior motive.'

'It was very nice of you, but——'

'Before you refuse there are a few other things you should know,' he put in firmly.

She swallowed hard, watching him warily.

'I've returned Gilbraith's ring,' Reece told her flatly.

Laurel gasped, her face paling, her hands shaking. 'No——!' she gave a strangulated cry.

His mouth tightened. 'Yes,' he nodded confirmation. 'Why didn't you tell me he was married?'

'I . . . You . . . you met his wife?' she choked, too distressed by what he had done to think straight.

He gave an abrupt inclination of his head. 'Gilbraith wasn't there, so I gave the ring back to her.' His mouth twisted. 'The most I can say for her is that she seems to care about their son,' he rasped.

'So now she knows about Giles and me?' Laurel groaned at this further humiliation.

'No,' he sighed. 'She thought I was from the police returning her stolen ring, and I didn't disillusion her once I realised who she was.'

'Giles told her the ring was at the jewellers,' she frowned.

Reece nodded. 'And then when he didn't get it back off you he told her the jewellery shop had been broken into and her ring one of the things stolen. You have to give him ten out of ten for ingenuity,' Reece scorned.

'You shouldn't have returned the ring, Reece,' she told him brokenly. 'Now I have nothing!'

His eyes glowed golden. 'You can't want a ring that belongs to Gilbraith's wife just because he gave it to you!'

'I *needed* that ring,' she cried, crumpling the envelope and the receipt in her hand.

'Why?' Reece asked softly.

She looked at him accusingly. 'You had no right to interfere.' Her voice broke as she dropped down on to the sofa. 'No right!' Her voice grew shrill.

'Tell me, Laurel,' he encouraged harshly. 'Tell me!'

She looked up at him with tear-filled eyes. 'I've lost it all now, Reece,' she sobbed. 'It's all gone! I won't take your money, and now I have no way of——'

'Of what, Laurel?' Reece urged forcefully as she broke off.

He knew. She was sure he knew without her having to tell him!

CHAPTER TEN

'How much did he take, Laurel?'

She breathed raggedly, her head down as she dejectedly accepted the fact that she had lost everything. How much had Giles taken? All that she was.

You could start again, a voice told her. With what, she mocked back. You're bright, that inward voice told her again, you know your stuff, you can make it. But she knew she couldn't.

'Laurel?' Reece prompted again.

She looked down at the crumpled receipt in her hands, reading out the amount from the bottom, to the last penny.

'Laurel——'

'Please don't touch me.' She cringed as he would have reached for her, her head going back proudly. 'Thank you for doing this for me, Reece, but no thank you.'

'Why not?' he ground out. 'If you insist on it you could always pay me back.'

'Oh, I'd insist,' she choked. 'But it wouldn't do any good. I make a living, I don't have enough spare cash at the end of the year to pay you.'

'Then take ten years, *twenty*!'

She gave a wan smile at his vehemence. 'No,' she refused dully.

'Why the hell not?' he rasped.

She shook her head. 'Mainly because I'm not

about to let someone else pay for my stupidity. I thought Giles was all that I wanted in a husband, that we would have a good marriage partnership.' She challenged him to question that description. He didn't. 'So I let him sign a few cheques for some of the bills, after all it looked as if I didn't trust him if I said no.' She bitterly recalled the way Giles had bristled indignantly when she had hesitated about agreeing to his offer to take some of the menial work off her hands before Christmas.

'He's a professional, Laurel,' Reece told her gently. 'Darling, he does this sort of thing all the time.'

Her head went back sharply. '*What?*'

Reece nodded reluctantly. 'I had my suspicions about the ring he had given you; it looked like a genuine antique. So I took it to a jeweller before going to Gilbraith's, he valued it at about five thousand pounds. That seemed a little excessive for a computer programmer,' he grimaced.

'Giles steals for a *living*?' Laurel gasped disbelievingly.

'Not all the time,' Reece sighed. 'He does actually have a legitimate job as a computer programmer. But he makes it a habit to prey on single women——'

'Gullible women,' she put in self-disgustedly.

'Vulnerable ones,' he amended firmly.

Laurel frowned. 'Are you just guessing or do you actually know all this for a fact?'

'I spoke to the police about the ring, and they were very interested in the fact that several of the

flats in your building have been broken into
lately——'

'Oh no!' she groaned protestingly.

'They have Gilbraith in for questioning now,
but from what I can tell, "oh yes",' he sighed.
'Your neighbour, the curious one,' he derided,
'has already confirmed that he came to your flat
the night it was burgled.' His eyes narrowed as
she blushed profusely. 'You already knew that,
didn't you?' he said in a puzzled voice.

She moistened her lips with the tip of her
tongue. What was the point of denying it now,
Reece already knew so much. 'He was looking for
the ring,' she revealed dully. 'The other inexpensive pieces of jewellery were taken to allay
suspicion.'

Reece frowned. 'But if you knew it was him
why didn't you tell the police? Me?' he added in a
hurt voice.

She shook her head. 'Does anyone really like
admitting they've been taken for a fool?'

'But it became so much more than that,
Laurel,' he rasped. 'Conning you out of money is
one thing,' he continued, even though she
winced at the word 'conning'. 'Breaking into
your home——'

'Twice,' she put in softly. 'He was there
when I got in two nights after the burglary,
when you found me at the shop at two o'clock
in the morning,' she explained at his questioning
look.

'Laurel, didn't it occur to you to be frightened
by the things that were happening?' he snapped
disgustedly.

'Of course it occurred to me!' she glared at him. 'Why do you think I moved in here?'

'So you could be closer to the only thing you care about,' he bit out harshly. 'The police will probably want to talk to you some time, but I told them they could probably find you here,' he scorned. 'You do intend spending Christmas with your books, don't you?' he derided.

'I haven't made any plans yet,' she muttered.

'I have,' he drawled. 'But I don't have the woman I want to share them with.' He turned away. 'In the meantime it looks as if I own the lease on a bookshop; do you know anyone who would like to run one?' he said bitterly.

'Reece——'

'If you do decide you would like the lease after all,' he picked up the receipt and put it back in his pocket, 'then I think I should warn you that it's an inclusive deal—I come along with it. You see, I'm not proud, Laurel,' he rasped. 'I can take whatever crumbs you give out. While you're thinking about it I would suggest you match notes with Amanda; I have a feeling some of your ideas about the past will be completely demolished!' He walked to the door, turning to see her surrounded by her cash books and the day's takings. 'This seems to be where I came in,' he sighed, the bell over the door telling of his departure seconds later.

No, it wasn't where he had come in, that had been on a treacherous night just over a year ago, and she had been fighting her feelings for him ever since. She had been instantly attracted to him, had known he felt the same way, and she had used the excuse of their parents' relationship to alienate herself from him. She had seen his puzzlement in her sudden cooling towards him, and she had congratulated herself for stopping what could have developed into a relationship that would ultimately cause her pain.

As it was now.

She could deny it all she wanted, but leaving Reece this morning had been the hardest thing she had ever done. Or was ever likely to do. Losing the shop was easy in comparison.

Dinner was a strained meal, with Robert making his excuses shortly afterwards, going to his study and leaving the two women alone.

Amanda smiled. 'He thinks I don't know he goes in there to have a cigar after dinner.'

Laurel accepted her cup of coffee. 'I didn't realise he smoked.'

'Just a cigar after dinner,' her mother said indulgently. 'He goes into his study because he knows I can't stand the smell.'

'Daddy smoked,' she spoke without thinking, looking up awkwardly.

'Yes, he did,' her mother nodded sadly. 'It was what killed him in the end. His health had deteriorated very badly before he had the heart-attack.'

Laurel's fingers tightened about her saucer. 'You seem to know a lot about it?'

'Dan,' Amanda supplied simply. 'He always kept me informed about your father.'

'Why?'

She sighed. 'I lived with him for twelve years,

Laurel, I still cared about the man.'

'You divorced him,' she accused.

'Yes,' she acknowledged sadly. 'It wasn't easy.'

'They why did you do it?' she scorned.

'Our love had—become something of the past, and trying to keep the relationship going was killing your father——'

'Not you?' she accused.

'Your father was not a man who liked to be tied to one woman,' Amanda carried on firmly. 'His first marriage ended in the same way, but to give him credit he stayed with me for twelve years. It was more than I had hoped for.'

'You were the one that asked for the divorce,' Laurel reminded hardly.

'I don't regret that decision for a moment, Laurel.' Amanda held her gaze steadily. 'The only thing I do regret is that you and Dan were hurt in the process.'

'You divided us down the middle just like you did everything else in the settlement,' Laurel bit out hardly.

'Do you really believe that?' her mother frowned, pain in her deep blue eyes.

'I *know* I went with you and Dan went with Daddy!'

Her mother shook her head. 'It didn't have to be that way——'

'It *was* that way!'

'Yes,' she sighed. 'But that was because it was the way Dan wanted it.'

'Dan?' she questioned sceptically. 'What choice did he have, either?'

'He was sixteen, old enough to decide where he wanted to go, *who* he wanted to go with,' her mother stated flatly. 'He chose your father.'

'Over me?' Laurel cried disbelievingly.

'Over both of us,' Amanda said in a pained voice.

'I don't believe it,' she shook her head.

'He'll be here for a visit soon, you can ask him yourself,' Amanda shrugged.

She frowned, puzzlement darkening her eyes. Dan couldn't have *chosen* to leave her. They had been so close, Dan always her champion, he couldn't actually have chosen their father over her.

'Laurel,' her mother spoke gently. 'He did what he thought best.'

'For *whom*?' she disclaimed.

'For your father.'

She shook her head. 'Then why couldn't I have gone with him, too?'

'Try to understand, Laurel,' her mother encouraged. 'Your father was never a man who liked responsibilities, and when I met him he had already been alone with Dan for six months, he desperately needed someone to take care of them both——'

'He loved you!'

'Yes, he did,' her mother agreed gently. 'But I've often wondered if we would have married at all if it hadn't been for Dan. He couldn't cope with him on his own, and his ex-wife wasn't considered a fit mother, and so we were married only three weeks after we met. Then we had you, and everything seemed to be going well. But your father began to feel trapped by all the domesticity. He was a man who really needed to be free, and by that time Dan was old enough to give him that freedom without leaving him completely on his own. Dan knew that. And, although I felt by that time as if Dan were my own child—he did call me Mum——' she reminded, 'I had to let him go.'

'But what about me?' It was a cry she had mentally made to herself a thousand times as a child, feeling unloved and unwanted by everyone.

'Darling, I would have let you go to them if I had thought your father could cope, even though it would have meant I had to give you up,' she added emotionally.

'I wanted to be with them!' she cried.

'Do you think I didn't know that?' her mother said in a choked voice. 'You withdrew from me, shut me out, flinched from me whenever I tried to cuddle you, until in the end I became afraid to reach out and touch you.'

'Afraid?' she scorned.

Anger flared briefly in the tear-wet eyes. 'Parents can be hurt too, Laurel,' she reproved huskily. 'I even asked your father if he would take you, explained to him that the strain of the divorce was having too adverse an effect on you. He thought it would be better if he got out of your life completely.'

'America,' she realised faintly.

Amanda nodded. 'I pleaded with him to reconsider, but it was no good. After he and Dan had gone you got worse. The only thing that made you in the least happy was books. So I bought them for you, hundreds of them, just so that I could occasionally see you happy once again.'

'It also kept me out of your way,' Laurel accused harshly.

'I didn't want you out of my way!' Her eyes flashed. 'I wanted back the warm, loving child I had always known. But she had gone—and she never came back.'

'What did you expect?' she derided. 'You dragged me about from place to place like a sack of potatoes!'

Pain once again darkened her mother's eyes. 'Are you ready to hear this, I wonder?' she sighed.

'I'm ready,' she nodded grimly.

'All right,' Amanda nodded. 'Did you notice anything else about those moves we made?'

She frowned. 'What sort of anything else?'

'Just—anything.'

'My toys disappeared,' she bit out.

'Yes,' her mother sighed. 'And each flat got smaller and smaller.'

'I don't remember.' She shook her head.

'I sold your toys, Laurel, just as I sold anything of mine that I could, too,' her mother told her in a rush. 'I needed the money, you see.'

'Why?' Uncertainty flickered in her eyes now.

She wet her dry lips. 'Once your father went to America the allowance he had agreed to pay us stopped coming.' She gave a ragged sigh. 'I kept writing to him, but—I think he just forgot we existed!'

'No!'

'Maybe he didn't.' Her mother shook her head.

'All I know is that the money stopped coming. And after being married and out of work for twelve years the only sort of job I could get didn't pay all that well. Once Dan was old enough to get a job he used to send us a few dollars every month——'

'You took money off Dan?' she said disbelievingly.

'I didn't want to,' she choked. 'But what little money we had seemed to go nowhere——'

'You still kept buying me books!'

'I went without lunches for those,' her mother said impatiently. 'They were the only thing that made you happy!' she defended again.

Years of building a wall about her emotions didn't make it easy for her to accept what Amanda was telling her, even though her mother had an explanation or reason for everything that had happened.

'Frank Shepherd used to—touch me,' she announced harshly.

Her mother paled, her eyes very dark. 'Oh no,' she gave a strangulated cry. 'Oh God, no,' she choked, the tears starting to fall.

Laurel watched her with detachment, still unable to release all the pent-up hatred she had for her mother. 'Reece told me to ask you why you divorced him?' she stated flatly.

Amanda bit her bottom lip. 'He—he was brutal with me,' she finally revealed raggedly. 'He was rich, and—and I wanted you to have the best again. He gave me money to buy you pretty clothes, to send you to a private school, and because I learnt of his cruelty as early as our honeymoon I decided a boarding-school would be best.' She looked at Laurel with beseeching eyes. 'He didn't—didn't——'

'No, he didn't do that. He talked mainly, but sometimes—sometimes he touched me, too.' And for years he made her believe she wanted only a coldly dispassionate, physical relationship with a man.

'No wonder you hate me,' Amanda said brokenly. 'I tried so hard to do what was best, but it just didn't seem to work out that way.' She shook her head. 'I took you away from the brother and father you loved above everything else, introduced you to the perverted gropings of another man. I think I would hate me, too, if I had done all that!'

It had to be like a sudden thaw after a severe snowfall, this sudden rush of emotion, the tears that fell and couldn't be checked, the wonderful warmth of being held in her mother's arms, of feeling cherished and loved by the soothing murmur of her voice.

She couldn't remember the last time she had allowed her mother to hold her like this, the two of them sobbing at the understanding they had unexpectedly found.

CHAPTER ELEVEN

'IF we don't stop now,' her mother attempted lightly, 'we're both going to look a soggy mess by the time Robert comes back.'

Laurel sat back, wiping the tears away with her fingertips, a little shy about looking at her mother again after their show of emotion.

'Look at me, Laurel,' her mother invited, smiling shyly when Laurel reluctantly did so. 'Maybe we should have done this years ago,' she said ruefully, dabbing at her cheeks with a tissue from the box on the table. 'Maybe I should have insisted that your father take you, even though it would have been like cutting off a limb, and maybe I should have tried harder to persuade Dan to stay with us——'

'No,' Laurel cut in firmly. 'I agree we should have talked earlier, but the fact that we didn't is probably more my fault than yours. I've been pretty unapproachable all these years, and I probably would have resented you just as much if you had let me go to Daddy. You were in a no-win situation.'

'Don't resent Dan for what he did either,' her mother encouraged. 'It broke his heart to be separated from you, but he didn't know how to explain.'

'I don't resent him. I—I just wish I'd known *why* he did what he did. We were like strangers when we met again,' she recalled brokenly.

Her mother nodded. 'He told me all about it, said that he didn't feel he could relax with you, that he could see how he had hurt you and he didn't know how to reach you any more. I think he's coming over in February to try again. And remember, Laurel, it's much harder for a person to let you go when they love you than it is to hang on.'

That was what Reece had been telling her when they parted. He wanted her but he knew he couldn't keep her when she wasn't willing to meet him halfway.

'How about you and Reece?' Her mother seemed to guess where her thoughts had gone. 'Is that an unsolvable situation?'

She stiffened, and then forced herself to relax. This was her mother, and after the years of conflict maybe they would never be really close, but she knew she *could* talk to her.

'Not if I love him,' she replied tautly.

'And do you?'

'I don't know!' Laurel shook her head. 'I didn't think I was capable of loving anyone, but—but I love you.' She made the admission huskily, so long since she had used the words to anyone.

'Thank you, darling.' Her mother squeezed her hand. 'I know how difficult that was for you to say. And feel,' she added ruefully.

'I've always loved you.' She frowned at the realisation. 'I just didn't understand, why you did the things you did.'

'I'm not sure explaining would have helped the

situation at the time,' her mother grimaced. 'But I think we understand each other a little better now, and—and maybe we can build on that.'

'I hope so,' she said—and meant it.

'What will you do about Reece?'

'Nothing,' she swallowed. 'For the moment. I have to think, find out if I'm worthy of giving him what he deserves.'

Her mother smiled. 'I'm sure you are.'

'But I'm not,' Laurel grimaced. 'And until I am . . .'

'I understand,' her mother nodded. 'And now that we have all that out of the way I insist that you stay for Christmas——'

'I couldn't——'

'Maybe I didn't say it firmly enough, Laurel,' her mother cut in firmly. 'I *insist* that you stay with us for Christmas.'

Blue eyes warred with blue until finally Laurel was the one to give a rueful shrug. 'If you had been as strict with me fifteen years ago I probably wouldn't have dared behave in the way I did!'

Her mother gave a bright smile. 'Does that mean you'll stay?'

'If you're sure . . .'

'I'm sure,' her mother said briskly. 'I'll just go and make sure your room is prepared.'

Laurel knew that her mother was also giving her a few minutes to herself, sure that the efficient staff here would always have the guest rooms made up. But they were both aware that she had found their conversation more traumatic than anything she had expected before coming here tonight.

As a child it had been so easy to blame her mother for all that had happened, but as an adult she should have seen that there were always two sides to any story. If her father had really wanted to be with her then no inducement on earth would have got him to make the move to America, certainly her mother would never have been able to make him go, as she had always accused her of doing.

And Dan. Poor Dan. No wonder they had been strangers when they last met, she had always secretly blamed him for leaving her, too. His holiday here in February promised to be a very emotional one!

But what of Reece? He must have known quite a lot of what had really happened in the past, of the wrong way she had interpreted it, and yet he had still been able to love her in spite of her bitterness and coldness.

But accepting that her mother loved her was one thing, allowing Reece into her life, her heart, was something else entirely. Having just had her heart and soul restored to one piece she wasn't sure she was ready to give them away again; her body had always been his for the taking! And she knew, no matter what he said to the contrary, that Reece would want them all or nothing at all.

'Can I offer you a brandy?'

She looked up into Robert's kind, concerned face, knowing he had been told what had just occurred between Amanda and herself. Amanda. Even that had been a form of defence over the years, a way of forcing Amanda out of the mother role. Considering the bitch she had been she was lucky her mother and Robert still wanted anything to do with her! What had her mother said, it's harder to give up than hang on? The whole of her cried out in agreement.

'I think he's at home if you want to go over . . .'

She blushed as she looked shyly at Robert. 'Am I that obvious?' she grimaced, wondering just how long she had been in love with Reece Harrington; probably from the moment he had pulled her out of her wrecked car! But she had been denying love in her life for so long that it had been easy to deny her love for him, too.

'Only to the people that love you.' Robert handed her the glass of brandy.

'Robert,' she chewed on her inner lip, 'Robert, how is it possible to love a person when you—when you get no positive feedback, when that person is totally cold and logical?' She looked at him intently.

'Don't be so hard on yourself, Laurel,' he said gently, understanding her completely. 'You aren't cold and logical, you're just wary. You're also very much in love with my son.'

'Yes,' she acknowledged dazedly.

'And he's always been in love with you.' He gave a rueful smile. 'I knew it from the moment he came home from the hospital after your accident. I've even managed to get some work out of him the last year,' he derided. 'He's been at the bank all hours, and his social life has been non-existent—except for those family dinners he was always pressing me to arrange.'

Half of which she had avoided coming to! Reece was right, he wasn't too proud to show her his love, and he deserved more than the crumbs she had been giving him. 'No women?' she frowned, knowing what a sensual man he was.

'No,' Robert confirmed. 'My son is a one-woman-man. I've been worried for him, but I'm relieved to see that is no longer necessary.'

The last was added enquiringly, and she put her glass down with firm determination. 'Would you tell—tell Mummy that I won't be staying the night after all.' It felt strange to call her mother by that intimacy again, but she had a feeling a lot of things were going to seem strange in her life from now on, not least of them being having Reece Harrington as a husband.

'Can I also tell her that you and Reece will be over for lunch tomorrow?'

She turned at the door. 'Keep your fingers crossed for me.'

He smiled. 'I won't need to,' he replied confidently.

Laurel wished she had the same confidence, but her palms were damp, her legs feeling weak by the time she had passed through the doorway that linked Reece's wing to the main house as she went in search of him. Robert was wrong, Reece wasn't at home!

She turned to rejoin her mother and Robert, stopping, before determinedly going into Reece's bedroom and closing the door.

She was sitting up in bed when he opened the

door, coming to an abrupt halt as soon as he saw
her. Laurel was well aware of the picture she
made, her bared breasts pert and inviting, the
rest of her body smooth and creamy. Reece
looked as if someone had just punched him!

'You know,' she put her book down to remark
conversationally, 'I've been giving some thought
to your predicament, and I've come up with the
ideal person to run your shop for you.'

Reece stiffened, a resigned look coming over
his face, the golden blaze of his eyes dulling to
brown. 'Oh yes?' he prompted uninterestedly,
turning to close the door behind him.

God, he looked tired, so very weary, still wearing
the business suit from earlier, pulling off the tie
now, a defeated droop to his shoulders as he turned
away to begin undressing. How she loved this man!

She resisted the impulse to run to him. 'Yes,'
she nodded. 'She's very capable, has a lot of
experience, I think she would be ideal.'

He looked sad as he turned to face her. 'You
don't have to do this, Laurel.' He made a gesture
towards her nakedness. 'The lease and the shop
are yours, I don't want them.'

'Oh, I wasn't talking about me.' She shook her
head at his stunned look. 'Polly would love the
opportunity to be in charge, and I think she
would be perfect.'

Reece looked as if someone had taken another
punch at him! 'Polly? But I thought——'

'Oh, I couldn't do it, Reece,' she dismissed
lightly, as if the very idea were ridiculous.

'Why the hell not?' he rasped. 'If you——'

'My husband wouldn't like it,' she cut in.

'Husband?' he frowned darkly. 'What husband? Laurel——'

'And then there's the children,' she continued. 'Half a dozen of them at least. We could even have started on the first one already,' she added softly. 'I know it's supposed to be modern but I'm afraid I don't approve of working mothers, not when it isn't necessary financially. I intend to spend a lot of time with our children, showing them they're loved, and telling them how wonderful you are.' Tears glistened in her eyes.

'Laurel, I don't have any idea what's going on——'

'I know.' She moved up on to her knees, the bedclothes falling off her completely. 'Isn't it wonderful?' she smiled.

His hungry gaze feasted on her. 'Beautiful. But——'

'Not me, Reece,' she chided indulgently. 'I'm talking about the fact that it's finally you that has no idea what's happening. For so long it's been me,' she told him huskily, all teasing gone.

Hope began to shine in his eyes. 'But now it—it isn't?'

She shook her head. 'I spoke to my mother, made my peace with her, and now I'd like to do the same with you.'

He swallowed. 'So—do it,' he invited gruffly.

She laughed nervously. 'I'm not sure I know how now the time has come,' she admitted ruefully. 'I never wanted to love anyone the way I love you.' She stopped him as he would have taken her in his arms. 'But from the night of that awful engagement party you've managed to repel all my dragons one by one.' She looked at him with her love shining out of her eyes. 'I always believed that the legends about knights and dragons were a myth, but you are my White Knight, Reece. And I need you so much.' She gave a wan smile of uncertainty. 'If I promise never to say "Bah" or "Humbug" do you think you could bring yourself to marry me?'

He sat down on the bed beside her. 'I don't know how I could ever have likened you to Scrooge,' he groaned, cupping her breast.

'Because I was as repressed as he was.' She held his hand against her. 'I doubt if I'll be able to change overnight——'

'Depends what sort of night it is,' Reece put in wickedly.

'What a terrible pun!' she winced.

He laughed softly. 'A man in love is allowed a few little foibles, such as bad puns. Better get used to them,' he advised.

'Does that mean you accept my proposal?' She looked at him intensely.

'No.' He lay her down on the bed beside him. 'It means you accept mine! Let's start the way we mean to go on.'

'Does that mean you're going to totally dominate me?' she teased, her arms up about his neck.

His leg moved sensually over both of hers. 'Whenever I get the chance,' he growled.

'We're expected for lunch with our parents tomorrow,' she warned at the glitter of intent in his eyes.

'We might make it—but then again we might not,' he grinned.

She didn't care if she never left this room again, if she just stayed in Reece's arms for ever. 'Have your wicked way with me then, sir,' she invited in the coyly apprehensive voice of a historical heroine.

'Does the hero then proceed to ravage the fair maiden?' Reece prompted with relish.

'Unless she ravages him first!' Laurel laughed at his surprised expression. 'Historical novels have changed over the years. Could I ravage you?'

'Every time,' he admitted gruffly. 'Does this mean the romantic books are going to come out of the cupboard?'

She nodded. 'I might even have a go at writing one myself. After all, I'm living with a real live knight.'

'Are you really serious about giving up the shop?' he frowned. 'I thought it was your life?'

'Maybe Polly wouldn't mind a part-time assistant for a while,' she shrugged. 'But other than that I have other plans for my life.'

'Half-a-dozen children,' he recalled in mock horror.

'Not until you're ready for them.' She lightly caressed the hair at his temple. 'I meant I shall be too busy loving my husband to want to go out to work. Will you mind having an old-fashioned stay-at-home wife? Maybe I'm a throwback but I can imagine nothing more fulfilling than being your wife and the mother of your children.'

His eyes glowed like pure gold. 'You can be whatever you want to be, my darling, as long as I can always be sure of your love.'

'There will never be any doubt about that,' she assured him, and meant it, intending showing him for the rest of their lives how much she loved him, knew that one day there would be another little boy with dark hair and golden-brown eyes to love and cuddle a tattered teddy bear called Fred, that that little boy would love the man at her side almost as much as she did. Almost. Because no one could love him as much, or more, wanting it all with him, knowing he would never hurt her or let her down, that *their* children would never know the trauma that she had.

She thankfully gave him her heart, her body, and her soul.

Harlequin Presents

Coming Next Month

Available in May wherever paperback books are sold, or through Harlequin Reader Service.

In the U.S.
P.O. Box 1397
Buffalo, N.Y.
14240-1397

In Canada
P.O. Box 2800, Postal Station A
5170 Yonge Street
Willowdale, Ontario M2N 6J3

No one Can Resist . . .

HARLEQUIN REGENCY ROMANCES

Regency romances take you back to a time when men fought for their ladies' honor and passions—a time when heroines had to choose between love and duty . . . with love always the winner!

Enjoy these three authentic novels of love and romance set in one of the most colorful periods of England's history.

Lady Alicia's Secret by Rachel Cosgrove Payes

She had to keep her true identity hidden—at least until she was convinced of his love!

Deception So Agreeable by Mary Butler

She reacted with outrage to his false proposal of marriage, then nearly regretted her decision.

The Country Gentleman by Dinah Dean

She refused to believe the rumors about him— certainly until they could be confirmed or denied!

Everyone Loves . . .

HARLEQUIN GOTHIC ROMANCES

A young woman lured to an isolated estate far from help and civilization . . . a man, lonely, tortured by a centuries' old commitment . . . and a sinister force threatening them both and their newfound love . . .
Read these three superb novels of romance and suspense . . . as timeless as love and as filled with the unexpected as tomorrow!

Return To Shadow Creek by Helen B. Hicks

She returned to the place of her birth—only to discover a sinister plot lurking in wait for her. . . .

Shadows Over Briarcliff by Marilyn Ross

Her visit vividly brought back the unhappy past—and with it an unknown evil presence. . . .

The Blue House by Dolores Holliday

She had no control over the evil forces that were driving her to the brink of madness. . . .

What the press says about Harlequin romance fiction...

"When it comes to romantic novels...
Harlequin is the indisputable king."
— *New York Times*

"...always with an upbeat, happy ending."
— *San Francisco Chronicle*

"Women have come to trust these
stories about contemporary people,
set in exciting foreign places."
— *Best Sellers*, New York

"The most popular reading matter of
American women today."
— *Detroit News*

"...a work of art."
— *Globe & Mail*, Toronto

Take 4 novels and a surprise gift FREE

WHAT READERS SAY ABOUT HARLEQUIN INTRIGUE . . .

Fantastic! I am looking forward to reading other Intrigue books.

*P.W.O., Anderson, SC

This is the first Harlequin Intrigue I have read . . . I'm hooked.

*C.M., Toledo, OH

I really like the suspense . . . the twists and turns of the plot.

*L.E.L., Minneapolis, MN

I'm really enjoying your Harlequin Intrigue line . . . mystery and suspense mixed with a good love story.

*B.M., Denton, TX

*Names available on request.